DECISION AT

A counterfactual his

Andrew J. Heller

DECISION AT ANTIETAM
A counterfactual history of the Civil War

**The Southern States on the eve of the
Civil War**

Introduction

The American Civil War is by all odds the single most popular subject of alternate history fiction in this country, just as it is the most popular subject of straight history in the United States. This popularity is doubtless related to the fact that there are many people, particularly in the Southern States who remain unreconciled to historic outcome of the war, even in the 21st Century. Indeed, the phenomenon has actually grown in both scope and seriousness, as Southerners have been joined by radical Libertarians and like-minded persons who have tried to set up the Confederate States of America as the 19th Century equivalent of a failed American Revolution, a noble, if ultimately doomed cause.

Many novels have been written in which the South was victorious, but until recently, the majority of these were dedicated to showing that Lee, Jackson, Stuart and their men were better than the Yankees, and deserved to win. In other words, they were for the most part, fairly harmless hero-worship.

Within the last 20 years or so, things have changed. A considerable number of revisionist "histories" of the Civil War by alleged scholars have been published, purporting to show that, among other things, secession had nothing to do with slavery, the war was entirely the result of Northern aggression, secession was justified by intolerable oppression of the South by the Federal government, and similar, equally dubious propositions.

This has in turn resulted in a series of new, openly political alternate histories of the Civil War which echo the afore-mentioned "scholarly" histories. These new alternate histories tend to be more strident in their claims of Confederate superiority, to the extent that many begin by assuming that the South would certainly have won the war if not for a terrible run of bad luck, such as the accidental shooting of Stonewall Jackson by his own men at Chancellorsville.

My purpose in writing this book is to show by means of a counter-factual "thought experiment" that if anything, the South was very fortunate to avoid being defeated much more quickly than it was in fact. The book begins by looking at what very nearly happened the Battle of Antietam in 1862, then goes on to use historical facts to explore the consequences that would have been likely to flow from what was initially only a very slight alteration in events (the late arrival of A.P. Hill at Sharpsburg). I have made every effort to base my conclusions on reliable historical sources, and done my best to set aside any preconceptions I may have had, although I cannot promise that I was completely successful with the latter.

I do not believe it is necessary to further prove that the Confederate cause was, in the words of Ulysses S. Grant, "the worst one men ever fought for", nor is this the place for it. My purpose here is to show that the South was, rather than the victim of unusually bad luck, the beneficiary of undeserved good fortune, and to offer a plausible example of how the war could have easily gone very much worse for the Confederacy than it did in fact.

Most of this book was originally published as part of a novel entitled *If the North Had Won the Civil War*, which was set in a 21st Century CSA. In retrospect, the counterfactual history may have been overlooked by serious students of the Civil War, because it was presented intermingled within a novel. So, for those of you who like your counterfactuals straight with no chaser, I give you *Decision at Antietam*.

In addition to some comparatively minor textual changes and corrections, and some additional argument in the Afterword, there is one major change from the original material. One criticism from even those comparatively few who souls who admitted to liking *If the North Had Won the Civil War*, was the lack of maps and other illustrations. I had accumulated many contemporary photographs of the (real) people places and things in the book, as well as a number of maps, none of which, for various reasons, were included in that book. I have taken the opportunity presented by the publication of this book to address that oversight, and I think the addition represents a significant improvement over the original presentation. All illustrations are in the public domain and courtesy of the Library of Congress, unless otherwise noted.

Andrew J. Heller
May, 2018
Erdenheim, PA

Robert E. Lee and his staff

Chapter One
"A most terrible sight"

Robert E. Lee began his invasion of Maryland in 1862 as he began all of his campaigns, with one goal in mind: to engage and destroy the enemy army in a single great battle:- in short, to recreate Napoleon's victory at Austerlitz.

The trait that made Lee notable among military men of his time and place was not his obsessive quest for a Napoleonic, war-winning victory in battle (this was typical of West Point graduates of his era), but rather his willingness to take long chances to achieve one. Napoleon's Grand Army almost always had numerical superiority and other tactical advantages over its foes in its great victories, particularly in artillery. Lee's Army of Northern Virginia, on the other hand, was normally outnumbered by its opponents, and if the Rebels possessed superiority in the cavalry arm, this was more than offset by the quality and quantity of the superb Federal artillery.

So in order to create the conditions for his Austerlitz, Lee had to take chances, sometimes what seemed like desperate chances. Like a professional riverboat gambler ready to risk his entire fortune on the turn of a card, Lee was willing to play with the highest stakes for the biggest prize, a war-winning battle of annihilation. While conventional military wisdom held that offensive action requires a manpower advantage of at least 3 to 2 in favor of the attacker, Lee repeatedly demonstrated his readiness to strike at the enemy in an attempt to bring about a battle of annihilation, undeterred by the fact that he was usually on the short end of 3 to 2 odds or worse.

Lee set the tone for his aggressive style of command in the first battle of the Seven Days, at Mechanicsville, by dividing his forces in the face of the much larger Union army in order to go over to the offensive. He left only 25,000 men in the Richmond defenses to face approximately 3 times as many Federals, while he shifted the bulk of his army across the Chickahominy Creek to gain local superiority, risking the loss of the Confederate capitol and possibly the war itself in an attempt to destroy the Union right wing.

When this blow went awry, he continued to attack the Federal army over the course of the following week, as if he had 105,000 men and the enemy 85,000, instead of the reverse. In the end, Lee was dissatisfied with merely defeating and driving off the bigger Union army, and saving Richmond. After the Seven Days, he wrote, "Under ordinary circumstances, the Federal Army should have been destroyed." Soon thereafter, Lee pushed all his chips in with another attempt to win the big pot, when he divided his army in the face of the enemy yet again, to bamboozle Pope and smash his army at Second Manassas.

It should be no surprise then, to discover that the characteristic which made Lee a great general would also be the one that led to his downfall. For if ever there was a design that involved the embracing of great risks, it was Lee's plan for the invasion of Maryland in September, 1862, designated Special Orders 191. Under this plan, the Army of Northern Virginia -- which after recent heavy fighting numbered fewer than 50,000 effectives -- was divided into several detachments, none of which could quickly come to the support of the others. The movements of these units moreover, would be made in the presence of a Federal army more than 75,000 strong.

Lee sent the bulk of his forces, consisting of 30,000 men divided into three units, under Brigadier General John G. Walker, Major General Lafayette McLaws and Major General Thomas J. "Stonewall" Jackson, with the latter in overall command, to surround the Union

14

garrison of 12,000 guarding the Federal armory at Harper's Ferry at the confluence of the Potomac and Shenandoah Rivers. Meanwhile, Major Generals Longstreet and D.H. Hill with 12,000 men, were given the task of preventing any Union forces from intervening by guarding the northern approaches to Harper's Ferry at Hagerstown and South Mountain. During this operation, the various units of the Army of Northern Virginia would be separated from each other by more than 20 miles, and would be unable to support each other in the event of any sudden, unexpected activity by the Union army. The entire movement was scheduled to begin on September 10, with the reduction of Harper's Ferry to be completed, rather optimistically as it turned out, by no later than September 13. As it happened, Jackson's men were not in position on the heights overlooking Harper's Ferry until the 15th, when the Federal garrison was forced to surrender.

Certainly Lee had his reasons for assuming that the Federal commander, George McClellan, would not make any sudden moves which might put the divided Army of Northern Virginia at risk. McClellan was a man who thought not merely twice, but repeatedly, before making a decision of any kind, and after the Seven Days, Lee had taken his measure. "He is an able general," Lee told one of his subordinates, "but an exceedingly cautious one." Moreover, "Young Napoleon" (one of McClellan's nicknames, and a singularly inappropriate one), constantly labored under the delusion that his army was outnumbered by Lee's, when in fact the reverse was true.

In addition, Lee believed that Army of the Potomac had been so badly mauled after the Seven Days that it would not be capable of undertaking offensive operations for at least another three to four weeks, by which time he expected the Federal unit at Harper's Ferry to be eliminated and the Army of Northern Virginia reunited. In this he was overly optimistic. The

Union army had recovered from the recent reverses in Virginia far more quickly than Lee anticipated, as he was to soon discover.

Still, perhaps everything would have fallen out as Lee had envisioned, but for the unlikeliest of accidents. A copy of Special Orders 191 had been used by one of D.H. Hill's staff officers to wrap some cigars, and the officer had carelessly mislaid the precious paper. On September 13, that copy of Lee's battle plan was found by two Union soldiers as they foraged through an abandoned Confederate camp outside Frederick, Maryland. Their discovery was in the Union commander's hands a few hours later.

McClellan was now in the position of a poker player who can see the other player's cards while his opponent suspects nothing. The Army of the Potomac, with more than 80,000 men, had the opportunity to attack and overwhelm the smaller Army of Northern Virginia while the latter was scattered in penny packets all over the landscape. Moreover, the Federal Army was closer to the various parts of the Confederate army than they were to each other. If he moved quickly, McClellan could destroy the smaller portion under Longstreet and D.H. Hill at Boonesboro, then descend on the remainder under Jackson's command, while they were engaged in the capture of Harpers Ferry, crushing each of the scattered units in detail with overwhelming numbers. In short, the Union commander knew he had a full house and that his opponent held a busted flush. All he needed to do was go all in on the pot, show his cards and the game would be over.

But George McClellan had risen to the top of his profession by his attention to detail and thorough preparation, not by risk-taking. He had almost nothing of the riverboat gambler in his make-up and even under these circumstances, when the war might be won with a forced march and an all-out attack, he moved cautiously.

16

He attacked the Confederates at Turner's Gap on South Mountain on the 14th, eventually flanking the outnumbered Longstreet out of the position only after a long day of fighting. By then, however, the situation had changed.

Lee was soon made aware of the lost orders, and of the dire peril of his army. Under the circumstances, the most logical move would have been for him to withdraw back across the Potomac, while sending new orders for Jackson to rejoin him in Martinsburg, where the campaign had begun. Given McClellan's record both before and after the ensuing battle, it seems unlikely that the Federal army would have pressed the Confederate retreat very closely. Why Lee did not call off the attack on Harper's Ferry and return to Virginia is still a matter for speculation. In the light of what followed, it must remain so forever.

Instead of abandoning the campaign and returning to his starting point, Lee chose to challenge McClellan, taking up a strong position in the little town of Sharpsburg, located in an angle between Antietam Creek and the Potomac River, and called on his army to assemble there. When he received word that the Federal garrison at Harper's Ferry had finally been forced to surrender on the 15th, he ordered Jackson to bring all his men to Sharpsburg as quickly as possible to join him.

What made Lee's decision so strange was that the coming battle would be a straightforward slugging match, with no opportunity for him to attempt the kind of dazzling maneuvers that had been the key to his previous victories. There was no possibility of an Austerlitz at Antietam; at least not for Lee. Given the disparity in numbers between the two armies and the nature of the position however, it might become a battle of annihilation with the Lee's army on the short end.

Even after all of Jackson's men arrived in Sharpsburg, the Army of Northern Virginia would be able to count no more than 47,000 men as "present for duty", not all of whom would be available if the battle began the next morning, as Lee expected. As it was, even though McClellan did not attack for two more days, packets of men, a division or two at a time, continued to arrive at Sharpsburg on the day of the battle, often just in the nick of time.

The high ground overlooking the Antietam Creek made for an excellent defensive position, but it was far from impregnable. And if the line was broken, there was nowhere for the defenders to go. The position backed on the broad Potomac River, with only one small ford available if a sudden retreat was required, a ford which was utterly inadequate to permit more than a handful of men at a time to cross. If the Federals did break through, the Army of Northern Virginia would be caught in a trap from which there was no escape.

Antietam Battlefield

McClellan arrived at Sharpsburg on September 15 and characteristically followed his instinct for caution, using the whole day for a long and careful inspection of the Confederate position before making any rash move, such as ordering an attack. On that day, Lee had fewer than 18,000 men against perhaps 55,000 Federals. Had McClellan attacked on September 15, the result could not have been in doubt. But he did not. In the end, this mistake worked in his favor, as the whole Army of Northern Virginia was caught in the subsequent disaster, instead of just a small part of it .

Stonewall Jackson and the larger portion of the Army of Northern Virginia began to arrive the next day. The Federal soldiers stood by and watched as the butternut columns continued to file into the position on the heights behind Antietam Creek throughout the day. The Army of the Potomac was still concentrating its divisions, and on the day of the battle the Union army would have 87,000 men available to fight the Confederate total of fewer than 42,000. McClellan opened the battle the following morning at dawn. It would prove to be the bloodiest single day of the war.

By the morning of the 17th, McClellan had gotten his opportunity for a good look at the enemy army, and could count their numbers for himself. The evidence of his own eyes assured him that, whatever phantom Southern armies had haunted him in the past, he was not outnumbered on this day, here at Sharpsburg. As he was not constrained by his customary nagging fear that he was about to be overwhelmed by superior numbers, McClellan felt himself in a position to commit his army to the attack. Still, even on this day of days, with Lee's army in the palm of his hand, the voice of caution would return to whisper in George McClellan's ear at the most inopportune moment.

The Federals opened the battle by sending Major General Joseph "Fighting Joe" Hooker's I Corps to attack the left of the Confederate line. Three divisions under Brigadier Generals Abner Doubleday, George Meade and James Ricketts were launched south along the Hagerstown Turnpike. The goal was the little white church consecrated to the Dunker faith located on the high ground overlooking the northern end of the Confederate line. If Hooker could take the Dunker church and the grove of trees surrounding it, then post a few batteries of artillery there, the Southern left would collapse, and the battle would be won.

In the gray light before the sun's disk had cleared the horizon, I Corps began its advance. Hooker's men quickly ran into a strong line of Southern infantry and artillery massed on either side of the turnpike in front of the Dunker Church, in a cornfield on the east side and a stand of woods on the west. I Corps met a hail of musket and artillery fire which broke the attacking column to pieces, and the bluecoats recoiled, leaving hundreds of bodies behind in the cornfield.

Hooker brought up a few dozen field-pieces, placed them on a ridge enfilading the cornfield, and swept it with deadly volleys of canister until, witnesses claimed, not one stalk of corn nor a single man remained standing. I Corps resumed its advance, on the verge of capturing the Dunker church, and with it, victory.

When all seemed lost for the defenders, out of a grove of trees by the church came Brigadier General John Bell Hood's Texas division, on the run. Their charge caught the unprepared Northern soldiers square in the flank, shattering their formations. A single great volley of muskets laid low hundreds more of the Federals, and their surviving comrades were forced to stumble back again across that terrible cornfield, which was covered with the still forms of men from both armies who had been killed there in the fighting earlier in morning.

Back went what remained of Hooker's men, all the way back to where they had jumped off at dawn. Hooker himself was out of action with a ball in his foot, his corps wrecked and incapable of further effort after losing 2,500 men dead, wounded or missing. The Confederate counter-attack was brought to a bloody halt by Federal guns, and the position stabilized, for the moment.

Now McClellan sent in the XII Corps under another Joe, the tough old Regular, Major General Joseph Mansfield. His men grimly retraced the steps of Hooker's men, taking heavy losses, including Mansfield himself, who was mortally wounded while leading the assault , but also recapturing the ground that had been lost. Back across that deadly cornfield the fight swept again, leaving behind more bodies to join the hideous piles of dead from both sides who already lay unmoving on the ground or sprawled across the split -rail fences bordering that blood-soaked plot of earth. In the end, the XII Corp's attack just reached the Dunker Church before it too shuddered to a halt, its ranks thinned by terrible casualties, its organization shattered from the loss of too many officers and the death of the corps commander.

McClellan had up to this point been utterly incapable of or unwilling to apply his two- to one advantage in numbers by attacking Lee all along the line simultaneously. Surely though, after seeing the near-success of his first two tries, he was now ready to use his numbers to overrun the Confederate position, attacking all along the line and crushing it with his army's weight of manpower.

But no, the sacrifices of first Hooker's men, then Mansfield's, had not changed Little Mac's (another of McClellan's nicknames) *modus operandi*. To put in all his men at once, to gamble all of his chips on one hand, returning for a moment to the poker table, would be to risk everything, and this ran directly counter to every fiber in McClellan's make-up . By feeding his men into action piecemeal, instead of going all-in with his attack, McClellan gave his adversary the chance to survive a fight against what should have been overwhelming numbers, permitting Lee to continually shift reinforcements from quiet sections to endangered ones, allowing him to put out the fires one at a time, rather than being consumed in a single, great conflagration.

McClellan now ordered the three divisions of Major General Edwin Sumner's V Corps across Antietam Creek to break the already shaken and depleted Confederate center. It was intended that the three divisions would go in side-by-side, but instead the attack was made one division at a time, stretching the defense to the breaking point, but never quite beyond it.

Major General John Sedgwick's division was in the lead. It advanced as far as the woods west of the Dunker Church before being taken in the flank and routed by fresh troops just arriving from Harper's Ferry. The second division, under the veteran Brigadier General William French, ran head-on into an extremely strong position: a sunken road held by Major General D.H. Hill's division, and backed by well-placed artillery. The road would acquire a new name that day: "Bloody Lane." French's men stormed the position in a series of headlong charges, and the attacks were torn to shreds, losing 1750 men in less than an hour and leaving the approaches to Bloody Lane carpeted with blue-uniformed bodies.

Sumner's third and final division, under Brigadier General Israel Richardson, now came up. Two regiments from New Yorker, the 61st and 63rd under Col. Francis Barlow discovered a knoll from which his men could enfilade the Southerners on Bloody Lane, and after a sharp fight in which Richardson was mortally wounded, Hill's men were driven off in a rout.

Had McClellan but seen it, the moment of victory was at hand: the center of Lee's line was well and truly breached. All that remained between the Federal army and the rear of the Confederate position was one regiment which was completely out of ammunition, a few dribs and drabs of infantry from used-up units and the remnants of an artillery battery which was so short of men that Longstreet's staff officers were working the guns.

On the other hand, available for McClellan to throw into the fight was his reserve of 13,500 men of V Corps (Major General Fitz John Porter). In addition, VI Corps under Major General William B. Franklin, with 12,000 more men had just arrived that morning. Franklin took one look at the situation and began to prepare orders for his troops men to advance in support of Richardson's division. Had he been allowed to issue these orders, it is difficult to see how anything but the destruction of the Army of Northern Virginia could have followed.

But McClellan did not see it. Instead of ordering Porter or Franklin to attack, he fell prey to the fears which had haunted him in earlier battles, and which now descended upon him at the critical moment of this one. With the aid of some bad advice from Porter (who reportedly told McClellan "Remember General, I command the last reserve of the last army of the Republic"), McClellan decided not to raise the stakes. Concluding that his own weakened right was in danger of a counter-attack by Confederate armies which existed only in his imaginings, McClellan ordered the protesting Franklin into a defensive position, and thereby gave Lee the time to close the gap in the center with fresh troops who had just arrived from Harper's Ferry. After that, it seemed as if the storm had passed, that Lee and his men had beaten the odds, and that the Army of Northern Virginia would live on to fight another day. But the Confederates were not in the clear just yet.

The IX Corps, under Major General Ambrose Burnside, was positioned on the extreme left end of the

Federal line. At around nine o'clock, McClellan ordered Burnside to cross the Antietam Creek and attack the Confederate right. IX Corps had been trying and failing to get over the creek all morning, in spite of having a huge advantage in numbers over the defenders. This was largely because Burnside, as brave and loyal as any man could be, possessed the tactical subtlety of a bull charging across a pasture.

He had interpreted McClellan's orders to mean that he was to seize a narrow stone bridge over the Antietam Creek (it could pass no more than four men abreast), and funnel all four divisions of his corps across it. The Rebel defenders had zeroed in on this unimpressive span, soon to enter the history books as "Burnside's Bridge", with sharpshooters and fieldpieces sited on the steep bluffs on the west side of the Antietam overlooking the bridge. The initial Federal attack by the 11th Connecticut was thrown back with heavy losses. A second try by two regiments from the First Brigade of the Second Division, was cut to ribbons before a Yankee soldier had even set foot on the bridge. In this way, 450 Georgians under the politician-turned-soldier, Brigadier General Robert Toombs, stymied 14,000 Northern attackers while the entire morning and early afternoon wore away.

BATTLE OF ANTIETAM—TAKING OF THE BRIDGE OF ANTIETAM CREEK.

Burnside's Bridge

As it turned out, the bridge was quite unnecessary. The Antietam is a shallow stream along most of its length, shallow enough in many places for a man to wade across without getting his trousers wet above his belt buckle. Indeed, after it was finally taken, Union soldiers found that they were able to ford the creek quite easily right next to Burnside's Bridge.

The corps commander would never have discovered this on his own, as he had not even considered the possibility of fording the creek, but fortunately for the Federal cause, Burnside had subordinates with somewhat greater mental agility than he. Brigadier General Isaac Rodman took his division downstream, to the Federal left, looking for an alternate crossing, and just after one o'clock he found one. His division crossed the Antietam at Snavely's Ford, and Union troops were now on the unprotected flank of the defenders.

At about the same time, back at Burnside's Bridge, a death-defying charge by two regiments of Irish shock troops, the 51st New York and the 51st Pennsylvania from Second Brigade (Brigadier General Edward Ferraro) of the Second Division (Brigadier General Samuel B. Sturgis) finally carried the bridge, braving heavy Confederate fire from as close as twenty-five yards away. (The Irishmen had been promised that their suspended whiskey ration would be restored if they took the bridge). Just like that, the seemingly impossible deed was done.

While the two 51sts were fanning out across their bridgehead on the west side of Antietam Creek, with more of the Ninth Corps pouring over the bridge behind them, Rodman's division appeared from downstream, and the slow Confederate withdrawal became a retreat, then a rout.

As it turned out, once Toombs' tiny force had been chased away, there was almost a vacuum in front of the IX Corps. The long delay in crossing the creek caused by Burnside's ineptitude had actually created a final and dangerous opportunity for the Union army. Lee had been thinning the right end of his line all day, seeing that the Union attack there was going nowhere, while the left and center had several times come close to being ruptured by Hooker, Mansfield and Sumner. Now, late in the afternoon, there were simply no reserves left to fill the void.

The result was that the road to Sharpsburg lay wide open in front of the IX Corps. If Burnside's men were not stopped, they would fall first upon the headquarters of the Army of Northern Virginia, then the flank and rear of the entire Confederate line on the far side of town, and it would all be over. It took some precious minutes for Burnside to re-organize the two divisions he now had across the creek, but by three o'clock, he was ready to renew the attack.

Lee, with his headquarters unit, a few hundred infantrymen from various shattered regiments and a handful of cavalry were now all that stood between the continued existence of the Army of Northern Virginia and disaster. Lee personally took command of this mixed bag of men, the shards of a number of broken units, most without their officers, forming them into the semblance of a line, and placed his staff officers in charge. They took up a position just outside of the southeast corner of Sharpsburg, with the left end of the line resting on the Boonesboro Road, and the right covering Harper's Ferry Road. Corporal William Lorch, a survivor of D.R. Jones's fragmented division, witnessed what followed.

"General Lee sat straight and tall on Traveller, as calm as if he was off to a church picnic. We could all see the masses of Blue infantry coming up the hill, directly at us. I cannot state their number with any degree of exactitude, but surely they outnumbered our little band many times over. An officer, a Major from his staff, I think, said something to General Lee, and gestured emphatically down the Boonesboro Road towards Shepherdstown. I believe he was urging General Lee to take flight in that direction. The General responded by shaking his head, and remaining in his place. General Lee pointed with his sword down the hill at the advancing Federal soldiers. 'Those people must be stopped. The entire army depends on it. Will you stop them for me, my brave men?' He asked in a high, clear voice. We all gave him a great cheer, and I cried out 'We'll stop them, Marse Robert!' along with all the others, although I knew in my heart that the only way they could be stopped was if the Almighty in His power stretched out His hand to preserve us, as He had long ago preserved the Israelites from the chariots of the Pharaoh. But I knew as well that I would have done anything for him, that I would have gladly laid down my life for General Lee. Any of us would done the

28

same. It seemed that only an instant passed, and suddenly they were upon us, a great multitude of blue soldiery directly before us and far overlapping either end of our meager little line. One of their officers barked out orders, and they shifted to a firing formation, with those in the front row kneeling to aim their muskets. A Captain from General Lee's staff shouted out orders, and we raised our weapons and fired a volley at close range, from no more than a hundred yards distance. We all cheered when many of the enemy sank lifeless to the earth as our Minie balls struck home. For the briefest heartbeat I dared to believe that the omnipotent Lord had seen fit to bestow upon our noble Army a miracle akin to the one He had granted to His Chosen People long ago. Then a sheet of flame erupted from the enemy line, as they responded with a volley incomparably greater than our own. Our line evaporated, vanishing like a tendril of smoke borne off by a vagrant draught. All around me my comrades had either been laid low, were fleeing for their lives or were casting their muskets to the ground in token of surrender. I had fallen to the ground, as the result of a ball through my right calf. As I lay prone, clutching my wounded limb, I saw General Lee, who still sat atop his noble horse Traveller, as calm and immovable as the marble image of a hero of old. Then I beheld a most terrible sight. Even after the passage of these many years, it still brings me great pain to recall it. The General gazed down, as if in perplexity, at a dark spot which had abruptly materialized on the left side of his breast. As he pressed his gloved hand to the wound, the stain began to extend rapidly in all directions, and a moment later I could see a dark fluid soaking into his glove. I did not doubt that I was watching the lifesblood depart his body. General Lee began to incline slowly forward, his eyes closing as if in token of a profound weariness, while his head sank to his chest. The Major astride the horse at his side reached out his hand, capturing the General's arm to avert a fall, but almost instantly more shots rang out, and at least three balls struck the Major at the same moment. He was hurled from his saddle with such violence that he seemed to fly backwards out of the saddle, over his mount's hindquarters. General Lee, now wholly deprived of support, sagged slowly down and to one side, then vanished from my view as he toppled from Traveller's back. I heard a despairing shout go up. 'They shot Marse Robert!' The Federals seemed to pause for a moment, as if realizing the significance of what had just occurred. Then one of them exclaimed, "Ol' Bobby Lee is dead!" and a great cheer went up, which was followed by many cries of 'Let's finish 'em...kill 'em all...' and the like..."

(From: **Ever Green in Memory: Recollections of a Soldier of the Army of Northern Virginia** by Reverend William Lorch)

Why did Robert E. Lee remain to be shot dead off the back of his horse by Burnside's men, when he had the opportunity to save himself from the wreck of his army? The question has been the subject of debate almost since the day the event occurred, a century and a half ago. Obviously, it is not one that can now be definitively answered, but there is enough evidence available to allow us to reach a plausible explanation.

Lee certainly understood that if the two divisions of the Union IX Corps were not held at bay, the only possible outcome of the battle would be the destruction of his army. There were simply no men available to guard the rear of the Confederate position on the other side of the village of Sharpsburg, and no place for the Army of Northern Virginia, trapped between the Union army and the Potomac, to retreat. Possibly he believed that the scratch line he had spliced together on the edge of Sharpsburg would be able to hold the Federals until help, in the form of A.P. Hill's division which was on the road from Harper's Ferry, could arrive.

This is probably not the true explanation. Lee was far too experienced an officer to believe that the hastily assembled stopgap line had any real chance to turn back two divisions of Burnside's men, or to even seriously delay them. It is far more likely that Lee saw that he could do nothing to avert the immanent destruction of his beloved Army of Northern Virginia, and that he intentionally chose to sacrifice his own life rather than survive to witness what he probably saw as a betrayal of his men.

Robert E. Lee was a man who was motivated by duty: duty to his country, duty to his home state, duty to his family, duty to the men he led. The men of the Army of Northern Virginia had given him their unconditional trust, and he had led them to disaster. For him, there were only two choices consistent with his sense of duty: either to surrender, and share the captivity of those of his men who survived, or to sacrifice his own life in a foredoomed attempt to save them. It is not hard to see how, for a man like Lee, the second was by far the more attractive of these alternatives.

The death of the Army of Northern Virginia followed closely on the heels of that of its commander. Burnside's men went through the little village of Sharpsburg and down the Hagerstown Road at a trot, overrunning the Dunker church at last, and smashing the Confederate position. There were a few minutes of bloody chaos in the Confederate lines as Longstreet tried to pull some men out to face the rear without thereby creating a gap for the massed Federals on the Hagerstown Road, but it was clearly hopeless. The Union men on the north side of town could see the Confederate position disintegrating before their eyes.

They gave a great cheer, and surged forward to the attack without awaiting orders from McClellan or their own corps commanders.

The situation was clear even from the opposite side of the Antietam Creek, where McClellan watched Lee's line melt away through his field glasses. It was so clear that he reversed his earlier orders, and peremptorily commanded Franklin to throw his 12,000 men into the battle. They were not needed, indeed, they were not even able to get into action before the fighting was over.

The Confederate forces were crushed, cut into disconnected segments and surrounded, their artillery overrun and turned on them, and many of their commanders killed or wounded. Hood died leading a death-or-glory charge; Stuart joined him, when he was knocked off his horse as he tried to organize a retreat across the inadequate ford; Jackson was struck down by a Minie ball that shattered his right arm. Union surgeons amputated the arm that night, probably saving his life.

In the end, Longstreet, the senior Confederate officer still alive and uninjured, had no choice but to surrender. He did so at 4:30, thus ending the bloodiest single day of fighting in the history of North America. It was also the most decisive day of the war, and the beginning of the end for the Confederacy.

By the time the guns fell still on the afternoon of September 17, 1862, of the 41,331 Confederate soldiers at Antietam, 13,872 were either dead, wounded or missing, with 39,175 (including the wounded) on their way to Northern P.O.W. cages. Fewer than 1,500 escaped the catastrophe. (Union totals of dead, wounded and missing were in excess of 16,000. The Army of Northern Virginia did not sell its life cheaply).

Almost as serious as the loss of men was the clean sweep of the army's generals, some of the Confederacy's most able officers. More soldiers could be found, perhaps, and another army raised to replace the one that had been lost, but who would lead it? Lee was acknowledged as being the one truly irreplaceable commander on either side. Dead along with Lee were the outstanding cavalry commander in the East, Jeb Stuart; the nonpareil fighter, John Bell Hood, and many others.

Still alive, but a prisoner and of no more value to the Confederate Army than if he had been killed, was Stonewall Jackson, the previously unbeatable leader of the "foot cavalry". With him into captivity went the steady, thoughtful, competent Longstreet, D.H. Hill and other irreplaceable leaders. The South had begun the war with superiority in two military categories which had offset, to some degree at least, the greater manpower, manufacturing capacity and more extensive rail system of the North. It had possessed a much more efficient cavalry arm and, in the Eastern theatre at least, it had the far superior leadership. After Antietam, the Confederates could no longer claim superiority in any important military category.

At just after 6 o'clock, ninety minutes after the last shots had been fired, A.P. Hill arrived at Sharpsburg on the Harper's Ferry Road with his division, the final piece of the now extinct Army of Northern Virginia. He had heard the news of the battle and of Lee's death from the handful of Confederates who had managed to slip away from the field, but he still brought his 2,000 men up to see if anything could be rescued from the wreck.

A.P. Hill

Whether the battle would have come out differently had Hill arrived two hours earlier, in time to stop Burnside's men is, of course pure speculation, but from that day forward, Hill believed that he could have at least saved Lee's life if he had driven his division harder up the road from Harper's Ferry. Hill took his men back to Richmond, and resigned his commission. He died a broken man in 1865, at the age of 40, haunted to the end of his life by his role in the disaster at Antietam. His last words were reported to have been "Just hold on, General Lee, I'm coming."

MAJOR GEN'L. GEO. B. McCLELLAN.

Entered according to Act of Congress in the year 1861, by M.B.Brady, in the Clerk's office of the District Court of the District of Columbia.

George B. McClellan

Chapter Two
"Under a dark cloud of impending doom"

Ironically, it was George McClellan, the least Napoleonic of generals, who was the victor in the most complete Napoleonic battle of annihilation of the war. After the Battle of Antietam, he was in a position to march on Richmond while the Confederacy had practically nothing with which to stop him, and thereby virtually bring the war to a close. He considered doing so during the next few days, poring over maps, holding councils of war with his corps commanders and drawing up plans to take the Army of the Potomac across the Potomac and back down to Virginia via the old Manassas battlefield.

A letter from Lincoln urged him to take precisely this step. The President praised him for his victory, but at the same time reminded the general that the fiasco of the Peninsula Campaign had not been forgotten by McClellan's enemies in Washington.

"You have won a great battle, one that history will rank among the supreme military victories of all time. It has given me the occasion for an announcement I had long wished to make, one that will plainly establish the moral basis of our cause before the world...[here the letter digresses into a long discussion of the purpose and anticipated effect of the Emancipation Proclamation, which was announced on September 22]
With this triumph, you have created an opportunity such as comes to a General at most once in a lifetime. You have shattered the enemy's army, which was both his sword and his shield, and in so doing have exposed his capital to capture, as it is now without any means of defense, and ripe to fall into your hands. You have only but to march boldly to take it,

and this terrible war which has torn our beloved nation asunder can be brought to a swift conclusion. Moreover, as you are deservedly the hero of the hour, your popular acclaim is at present so prodigious as to silence your ill-wishers here for the moment. But, if you do not press on to gather in the fruits of your victory, those detractors will unquestionably regain their voices, and I will be unable to staunch them.

I do not ask for any detail of your plan of campaign, as I place my complete confidence in the victor of the Battle of Antietam. If there is anything your Army lacks which might forestall immediate action, whether it is additional horses, men, guns, provisions, in short, anything, you need only to name it, and you shall have it as quickly as it can be supplied. I ask only that you act with all possible speed, before the enemy has recovered from the blow you have administered sufficiently to gather a new army to protect Richmond from capture.

On behalf of a grateful nation, I thank you for the historic victory you have given us, and for the ones that I am confident you will add to it in the future.

Your friend,
Abraham Lincoln"

(From **The Collected Letters of Abraham Lincoln**, John Hay, ed.)

But in spite of this encouragement from his Commander-in-Chief, in spite of his own initial impulse to follow up the victory with a rapid advance on Richmond, in spite of the urgings of his subordinate generals and the enthusiasm of the ordinary soldiers of the Army of the Potomac for finishing off the Rebels, in the end, he did nothing. The aggressive, energetic McClellan who had emerged just before Antietam now retired, to be replaced by the more familiar precise, cautious, careful version. By September 25th, a week after the battle, he was writing to Lincoln "…a premature advance at this time would place this Army, and thereby the country, in grave peril…"

Two days later in another letter to the President, McClellan insisted that the Confederates had a vast army of 150,000 men waiting to ambush him at Manassas, and that he could make no move of any kind until he had been reinforced with an additional 100,000 infantry, 10,000 cavalry and provided with a long list of supplies, from guns, to wagons, to bridging equipment. He wrote, "…if the Government refuses provide these absolutely essential requirements, I cannot be held responsible for the consequences." Finally, he suggested that he be restored to the top command in the Federal Army, replacing Henry W. Halleck as General-in-Chief, "… as the safety of the country requires a steady, competent hand at the controls."

By the end of September, it was becoming clear to Lincoln that McClellan had no intention of pressing the Confederates during the good campaigning weather that remained before winter set in. On October 1st, Lincoln left Washington and went down to see his commander at Harper's Ferry, hoping that a personal visit from the Commander-in -Chief would impress upon him the importance of immediate offensive action. This three day visit accomplished nothing.

After he returned to Washington on October 4, Lincoln instructed Halleck to order McClellan "…to cross the Potomac, and give battle to the enemy…Your army must move now, while the roads are good…"

McClellan responded to this direct order from his superior officer with yet another list of requisitions for supplies of every kind, which he said were absolutely essential before he could make any move. All through October, during perfect campaigning weather, the Army of the Potomac remained in camp, giving the Confederacy precious time to pull together an army to defend its capital. By the beginning of November, Lincoln had good reason to wonder whether Young Napoleon would ever move." [McClellan] is an admirable engineer," Lincoln told a visitor to the White House, "but he seems to have a special talent for the stationary engine."

It had been widely predicted that the Republicans would suffer a serious drubbing at the polls in the mid-term elections , due to growing unpopularity of a hitherto unsuccessful war. However, the Federal victory at Antietam made the Democratic claims that the war was a failure look hollow, and as a consequence, the opposition party gained only a handful of seats in the House, and none at all in the Senate. With the election safely behind him, and his party's control of the government undiminished, this should have been the moment for the President to sack his fractious general, as Secretary of War Stanton and the leaders of the Radical Republicans urged him to do. But still he hesitated. Why?

There were several reasons. For one thing, McClellan was still a hero to the general public and, to a somewhat lesser extent, to his army, as a result of Antietam (the soldiers understood that the victory was more in spite of Little Mac's generalship than because of it). Moreover, if Lincoln relieved McClellan, with whom would he replace him? It was not as if he had a Napoleon or a Wellington waiting in the wings to take over the Army of the Potomac. Finally, there was the undeniable fact that somehow, McClellan had defeated Robert E. Lee, and destroyed his army, winning the most complete victory of the war. Perhaps he could catch lightning in a bottle again, win another great battle, and bring the war to a close.

But before he could win the war, Little Mac would have to break camp and take his army down to Virginia to fight. As the days, then weeks, then months continued to go by, it became increasingly clear that, in spite of first suggestions, then orders to move, McClellan had no intention of doing anything before spring.

At last, Lincoln's patience ran out. On December 14, he told Halleck to order McClellan to "commence offensive operations with your army, beginning no later than December 21...", adding that if this order was not obeyed, McClellan would be relieved of his command.

This order did not have the desired effect on the general, possibly because he had already disregarded similar peremptory orders on several previous occasions without any repercussions. On December 15th, he wrote to his wife:

"They would gladly sacrifice this gallant army [by forcing him to move prematurely],if by doing so they could rid themselves of me, but I will not allow them to do it. The gorilla [McClellan's nickname for the President], Stanton and the whole rotten gang of nigger-loving politicians may bluster and threaten, but they are cowards and will do nothing in the end, as they are justly afraid of what the country would do to them."

(From **Reluctant Warrior: the Life of George B. McClellan** by Bruce Catton)

McClellan went so far as to air his feelings about the December 14 order over dinner with his corps commanders, saying, "Someone should take an army up to Washington, and clean out that nest of snakes," with the implication that the "someone" would be McClellan himself. This remark prompted General Burnside to call his superior a "traitor", then abruptly leave the table to write a letter to Washington in which he reported McClellan's indiscretion.

This time, McClellan had overestimated the strength of his position and underestimated the determination of the President. On December 21, 1862, President Lincoln carried out his threat, rewarding the man who had rescued his party at the polls with his victory at Antietam by relieving him of command, and replacing him with the senior corps commander of the Army of the Potomac, Major General Ambrose Burnside.

From that day forward, the sands of time, which had stopped flowing against the Confederacy for three months after Antietam, began to run through the hourglass once more. No one had ever accused Ambrose E. Burnside of being a military genius, nor was anyone more aware of his shortcomings as a general than the man himself. He had accepted the top command with the greatest reluctance, primarily to prevent it from being given to Joseph Hooker, a man who he detested personally and distrusted professionally. But Burnside had one quality which Lincoln required above all others: he would not hesitate follow orders from his superiors. And, if those orders were to cross the Potomac and invade Virginia, then he would carry them out to the best of his admittedly limited abilities.

Perhaps even more important than Burnside's willingness to obey orders from Washington was the readiness of the soldiers of the Army of the Potomac to follow their new commander. There had been some fear that the dismissal of the beloved McClellan might cause the army to mutiny, or at least seriously undermine its morale. But in the event, the soldiers gave the departing Little Mac a rousing round of cheers, then quietly adjusted to the new reality.

Burnside was a known quantity, and well-liked in the ranks. He was solicitous of the welfare of the ordinary soldier, and had a reputation of being brave, honest and patriotic. Moreover, the change at the top almost certainly meant that waiting was over, and the Army of the Potomac would soon have another opportunity to come to grips with the Rebel army, with the prospect that Richmond might be captured and the war brought to a timely end. Judging by their letters home at this time, the rank and file of the army were eager to follow up their hard earned victory at Antietam by handing their enemies another beating .

It was true that no-one had ever mistaken Ambrose Burnside for Napoleon Bonaparte, but then, given the disparity in numbers between the opposing armies, perhaps military genius would not be required. It might well be that under these circumstances, dogged persistence was all that was needed.

In Richmond, the news from Antietam was at first received with disbelief. Later, after the scope of the disaster had been confirmed, there ensued a combination of panic and dee despair. Special editions of newspapers containing accounts of the battle and the death of Lee were printed with black borders, like mourning letters. When Lee's remains arrived in Richmond on September19th (his body had been recovered from the battlefield and sent across the lines under a flag of truce by order of Lee's old Mexican War comrade, George McClellan), the population of the city went into a paroxysm of mourning for both the fallen hero and his lost army

.

Jefferson Davis

Jefferson Davis spoke after Lee's funeral, ostensibly on the subject of a cemetery that he promised to have built on the Antietam battlefield after the war's end, dedicated to Lee and the men he had led who had fallen there. In reality, the speech was intended to rally his shaken people in this, their darkest hour.

"… we will dedicate a portion of that battlefield to those who gave their lives that a nation might live.

But in a larger sense, we can never dedicate, we can never consecrate, we can never hallow that ground. The brave men who died there have consecrated it far beyond our poor power to add or detract. It is rather for us, the living, to be dedicated to the unfinished work for which they fought, that from those honored dead we take increased devotion to that cause for which they gave the last full measure of devotion. We here highly resolve that those dead shall not have died in vain, and that liberty shall not perish from the earth."

(From the **Richmond Dispatch**, September 20, 1862)

This speech, although it is considered to be the best Jefferson Davis ever made, did not solve his most pressing problem: the lack of both a commander and an army for him to command to oppose the expected Federal advance upon Richmond.

The commander at least was at hand. By the middle of October, General Joseph Johnston had recovered sufficiently from the wound he had received in May at the Battle of Seven Pines to return to active duty. Although he and the President cordially disliked each other, Davis overcame his personal animus to appoint Johnston on October 20 to the command of an army which, at that moment, could scarcely be said to exist at all. All that was available to defend Richmond were approximately 2500 cavalry and fewer than 10,000 infantry to oppose the Army of the Potomac which, on that day, had listed as "present for duty" more than 130,000 men. The President, General Johnston, the newspapers and the citizens of Richmond all anticipated the arrival of the blue-coats in overwhelming numbers any day.

"The entire city lives under a dark cloud of impending doom which affects one and all as if a literal cloud was lingering over the city, obstructing the rays of the sun, and condemning the inhabitants to perpetual darkness. It is impossible to take pleasure in food, drink, conversation or any other thing while rumor has the enemy approaching closer by the hour. Each day that passes without the appearance of the enemy at the gates does not bring a rise in our spirits, as might be expected. Instead, the gloom becomes even more profound, as the probability that the invaders will arrive the next day increases..."

(From: **Diary of a Senator's Wife** by Fanny Gilchrist Baker)

As it happened, fear of the Union army in the Southern capital was premature. Thanks to its commanding general, the Federal army made no aggressive movement of any kind for twelve weeks after Antietam, giving the Confederates time to pull troops from other theatres and cobble together a force that would have some chance to successfully defend Richmond.

But from where were these men to come? Relatively near at hand were approximately 12,000 men stationed in North Carolina none of whom were presently engaged with the enemy. However, most of these men could not be spared from the crucial duty of guarding the Wilmington and Weldon Railroad. This vital artery was the only direct rail link between Wilmington, North Carolina, which was by 1862 the largest operating Confederate port on the Atlantic, and Richmond. Earlier in the year, a Federal amphibious operation had penetrated Albemarle Sound and nearly cut the Wilmington and Weldon at the town of Goldsboro before being driven off. If too many men were taken from its defense, a renewed attack by Union troops could easily overrun Goldsboro, and sever this critical rail line.

There was really only one place where sufficient numbers of men could be obtained, and that was from west of the mountains. Unfortunately for the Confederacy, by the middle of October, 1862, the western armies were in no condition to spare any troops at all.

***

The first half of 1862 had been a catalogue of disasters for the Rebels in the West. Defeats at Ft. Donelson, Shiloh and Island Number 10 had led to the loss of more than 30,000 of men killed, wounded or taken prisoner, including the death of the theatre commander, Albert Sidney Johnson. The Federals had occupied all of Kentucky and most of Tennessee, and their gunboats penetrated far down the Cumberland and Tennessee Rivers to northern Alabama. A Union salt water fleet under Commodore Farragut had taken New Orleans in April, closing most of the Mississippi to the Confederacy, and a river squadron had captured Memphis in June. The Northerners had a manpower advantage of nearly 2-to-1, and if Halleck, the commander in the West, had kept up the pressure, there would have been very little the Confederates could have done to stop him.

Fortunately for the Southern cause, Henry Wager Halleck was a man cut from much the same cloth as McClellan. Although he had made certain that most of the credit for the Union successes in the West had gone to him, in fact the string of Northern victories in that theatre was primarily due to the initiative of intelligent and aggressive subordinates.

Halleck was himself was the least aggressive of generals. After occupying the railroad junction at Corinth at the Tennessee-Mississippi border at the end of May, he allowed the Confederate army there to pull out without making the slightest effort to pursue. Then, he split his huge force of 120,000 men into small detachments, putting most of them to work on routine occupation duties, rebuilding railroads, bridges and so forth.

The main Union effort of the summer was given to 40,000 men of the Army of the Ohio under Major General Don Carlos Buell, who was ordered to drive the Confederates out of Chattanooga and occupy eastern Tennessee. Buell, like his chief Halleck, and his old West Point classmate, McClellan, did not believe that wars were won by great battles, but rather by careful maneuvering. He therefore advanced slowly, taking care to avoid being surprised. Moreover, his army was dependent on the railroads for supplies, and Confederate cavalry raids by Nathan Bedford Forrest and John Hunt Morgan destroyed track, burnt bridges and blew up tunnels in his rear so effectively that, by the end of July, a total of 2500 Confederate cavalry raiders had brought Buell's 40,000 man army to a complete stop, still well short of Chattanooga.

GEN. DON CARLOS BUELL,

Entered according to Act of Congress, in the year 1862, by Jas. E. McClees, & B. W. Addis, in the Clerk's Office of the Dist. Court of the United States, for the Eastern District of Pennsylvania.

Don Carlos Buell

These delays gave the Confederates an opportunity to turn the tide of the war in the West. The new theatre commander in Tennessee, replacing General P.G.T. Beauregard, was General Braxton Bragg. He devised a bold, double-pronged offensive into Kentucky, hoping to recover the strategic initiative in the West, and force Buell to retreat back to the Ohio River. Bragg also expected the appearance of a Confederate army in Kentucky to bring in thousands of new recruits and revive the Confederate cause in this key border state.

For his campaign, Bragg had 32,000 men available under his direct command in Chattanooga, and 18,000 more under Kirby Smith further east, based in Knoxville. Bragg planned to rendezvous with Smith in Kentucky, and there fight a decisive battle with Buell, if and when the opportunity presented itself.

The risks were considerable: if Buell was able bring his entire army to bear on either Confederate column before they could join hands, the plan might easily end in disaster. If defeated in Kentucky, far from home or help, the Rebel armies might be swept off the board as completely as the Army of Northern Virginia would later be at Antietam. If that happened, the chances of the Confederacy's surviving another twelve months would be too small to consider.

The campaign started promisingly, with the Confederates getting the jump on Buell. Smith began first, leaving Knoxville on August 15, bypassing an 8,000 man Union division which was holding the Cumberland Gap, and reaching Richmond, Kentucky two weeks later. There he smashed a green Union division of 6,500 men, killing or capturing practically all of it . Smith went on to establish control over central Kentucky from his base in Lexington, installing a Confederate governor in the nearby state capital at Frankfort. He then settled down to wait for the arrival of Bragg, passing the time by printing and distributing pamphlets calling for Kentuckians to rise up and throw off their Northern oppressors.

Bragg took longer to get started, not getting underway until August 28. Even so, he was able to steal a march on the slow-moving Buell, so that by September 7, his army was in Glasgow, Kentucky, and closer to Louisville than the Army of Ohio was, with no substantial Union forces between him and Kirby Smith. Bragg's plan, which had seemed so chancy at the outset, now began to look better by the day.

Buell moved cautiously, uncertain of Bragg's goal. He reached Bowling Green, Kentucky at about the same time that Bragg entered Glasgow. He was pelted with frantic telegrams from Washington ordering him to move faster, to close with Bragg, and engage him in a battle. Lincoln found the general's response to these orders so unsatisfactory that he ordered Buell to be relieved, and command turned over to his senior subordinate, Major General George Thomas. Thomas declined, saying that it would unfair to replace Buell on the eve of battle, thus giving his superior a temporary reprieve pending the outcome of the battle. However, as an indirect result of the events at Antietam, the anticipated battle never took place.

The Confederate campaign could already have been considered a success, as it had seemingly regained everything that had been lost in Kentucky over the course of the winter and spring. All that remained to crown the campaign was for Bragg and Smith to unite their armies, smash Buell in battle, then bring Kentucky into the Confederacy.

Realistically, the likelihood of such an outcome had never been very great. Even after the two Confederate armies were combined, they would have had only a bare equality of numbers with the Army of the Ohio. Moreover, alarmed Republican governors of Ohio and Indiana had been rushing fresh troops to Louisville, and

50

two more divisions had been hurried to Buell's assistance from Grant's army in the west. Soon, the invaders would be outnumbered by a ratio of 3-to-2, or more.

As it happened, the campaign ended with a whimper, rather than a bang. The news of the disaster at Antietam reached Kentucky on September 20, along with new orders from Richmond. Bragg and Smith were directed to return to Tennessee immediately. Smith was instructed to detach 8,000 men from his force and Bragg 15,000 from his, for service in the new army forming under Johnston in the East. By October 4, Bragg and Smith were back in Knoxville, and over both generals' vociferous protests, 23,000 of their men were loaded on trains and shipped off to Richmond.

Bragg wrote to Jefferson Davis, warning the President that his depleted forces were now incapable of resisting a determined Federal offensive:

> "The enemy's numerical preponderance is now so great that the number of men remaining in my command is utterly insufficient for the task of defending Tennessee, and all of that State must be abandoned to the enemy the moment he chooses to move South in force. After that, if no reinforcements are forthcoming, he will be free to invade Alabama or Georgia almost as he pleases, as we will be without the means to do much more than harass him..."
> (From: **The Generals of the Confederacy: A Study in Command** by Russell Weigley)

Jefferson Davis was not a fool: he well understood the perilous military situation in the Western Theatre. His dilemma was that he had no reinforcements to send to Bragg. Indeed, he was under pressure to take even more men away from him than he had already.

Davis' new commander in Virginia, Joseph Johnston, was also demanding more men. He could hardly be blamed. Even with the additions from Tennessee, Johnston would still have only have 38,000 men to meet the Army of the Potomac with almost 130,000. Johnston told Davis that he would not be able to mount a successful defense of Richmond without a minimum of 20,000 additional infantry.

As was the case with Bragg, the President did not venture to disagree with Johnston's assessment. The trouble was, he did not have anything like 20,000 men to give Johnston. In fact, he had virtually none at all. For the moment, until new levies could be raised and trained, the cupboard was bare. The next time the Federals moved on Richmond, they were going to enjoy a nearly insuperable numerical advantage.

All that was keeping Southern cause alive was the absence of a Union commander willing to use his advantage in numbers aggressively. The Confederacy had been unduly fortunate in the early months of the war, facing men like Halleck, Buell and McClellan. But the roster of opposing commanders had changed, and new men, among them ones willing to hazard their armies in battle, were coming to the fore.

In the east, the new commander of the Army of the Potomac, Ambrose Burnside, was readying his men for a new offensive into Virginia. If at times he appeared to be a bit of a blockhead, he at least did not suffer from McClellan's delusion that he was constantly outnumbered. Burnside believed he had at least twice as many men as Johnston, and he was determined to use them.

In Tennessee, the Federal Army of the Ohio had a new man at the top as well. Buell's failure to vigorously pursue Bragg and Smith after they withdrew from Kentucky was the last straw for Lincoln. He was replaced by Major General William Rosecrans on October 2nd (Thomas, who had declined the command once, was not offered it again).

The most significant change was the one placed a new commander in charge on the Mississippi when Halleck was called to Washington. This Union general had already displayed the aggressive instincts which had resulted in victories at Ft. Donelson and Shiloh. With the help of his equally aggressive subordinate, William Tecumseh Sherman, he was now about to make plain the true military weakness of the Confederacy after Antietam in a way that could not be mistaken. His name was Ulysses S. Grant.

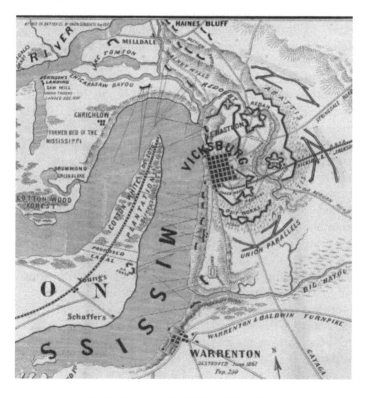

Vicksburg and its Fortifications

Chapter Three
"Vicksburg is ours and fairly won"

As 1862 drew to a close, disaster threatened to overtake the Confederate cause both east and west of the Appalachians. In the Eastern Theatre, Joseph E. Johnston was preparing the newly-formed Army of Virginia for a desperate defense of Richmond with the knowledge that he would be facing more than two-to-one odds in the coming campaign.

In Tennessee, Braxton Bragg with only 28,000 men, could do little but wait to see what his counterpart, Major General William Rosecrans, the new commander of the renamed Army of the Cumberland, with more than double his numbers, would do. Bragg did not even have the option of striking at the Federal supply lines with cavalry raids, the tactic which had stymied Buell's advance on Chattanooga, as most of his cavalry had been sent to the Eastern Theatre to replace the near-total loss of Jeb Stuart's cavalry at Antietam. The cavalry he had remaining were too few to operate effectively as independent raiders, and in any case Bragg felt that he needed them as scouts. Moreover, Bragg's best cavalry commander, Nathan Bedford Forrest, had gone east along with most of his men.

Further west, Grant had concentrated 38,000 men at Grand Junction, Tennessee, organized in three divisions under Major-Generals William T. Sherman, Charles S. Hamilton and James B. McPherson. His goal was Vicksburg, Mississippi, and he was in a hurry to get there for various reasons, not all of which were strictly military.

An ambitious Illinois Congressman named John McClernand had gained the approval of President Lincoln to raise a new army of volunteers from his home state, Indiana and Iowa, lead it down the Mississippi to take Vicksburg and "open navigation to New Orleans."

Along with this permission, he was given a commission as a Major-General. Grant feared that if McClernand's expedition reached Vicksburg before he did, he might be superseded in command of the theatre by this politician-turned-soldier. Therefore, as soon as he received permission from Halleck (who had no more use for McClernand than Grant did) in Washington to proceed, Grant hurried forward preparations for his campaign against the newly appointed commander of the Confederate Department of Mississippi, Lieutenant General John Pemberton.

Pemberton was a Yankee, and therefore something of an anomaly in the Confederate Army. He had been born in Philadelphia, and had spent most of adult his life stationed in various posts in the North. But in 1848 he married Martha Thompson of Norfolk, Virginia, and when that state went out of the Union in 1861, Pemberton put his love for her over his love for his country, by resigning his commission and joining the Confederate Army in March, 1861. Because of his northern birth, Pemberton was distrusted by a number of important Confederate politicians, although Jefferson Davis was not one of them.

Pemberton had been given the task of defending Vicksburg, which Jefferson Davis called "the nailhead that holds the South's two halves together." What he was not given was more men. Altogether, Pemberton's new department included roughly 50,000 men, but fewer than half of these could be used in the defense of Vicksburg. 26,000 of them, under the command of Major Generals Sterling Price and Earl Van Dorn, had come from Arkansas and Missouri, and were anxious to return to their homes west of the Mississippi, especially after hearing rumors that a new Union offensive into Arkansas was in the works.

Jefferson Davis advised Price and Van Dorn to cooperate with Pemberton, but did not order them to do so, and so in the end, they re-crossed the Mississippi, leaving Pemberton with fewer than 25,000 men to hold open the only connection between the two halves of the Confederacy, the stretch of the Mississippi between Vicksburg and Port Hudson.

At about the same time he learned he was losing half of his men, Pemberton was receiving news of McClernand's impending expedition, and discovering that Grant's army would soon be joined by another one just as large. Under the circumstances, he saw no choice but to take the field and try to defeat Grant before the numbers against him became impossibly one-sided. He wrote to Jefferson Davis to explain his thinking:

"To fortify Vicksburg, to stay inside the works with all of my men, and there await the Federal onset passively, would be to concede defeat and the loss of Vicksburg. My soldiers are brave, loyal and filled with fighting spirit, but they are simply too few to withstand the numbers that will ultimately be brought to bear if Grant and [McClernand] are allowed join forces. Once Federal siege works are drawn around Vicksburg, and we are pinned inside its fortifications, the outcome can only be a matter of time. I therefore propose to leave only a small force to defend the City, and bring the greater part out to engage in a war of movement. I will look for Grant to become careless, as has happened on more than one occasion in the past, and thereby leave open an opportunity for us to surprise and overwhelm an isolated detachment of his army, using as my model General Jackson's campaign in the Shenandoah Valley last spring."
(From **Heart in the South: The Biography of General John Pemberton** by Otis Carlsen)

In theory, this was an excellent idea; in practice however, it did not turn out so well. In part, this was because Pemberton was no Stonewall Jackson, and Ulysses S. Grant was neither a Fremont nor a Banks, but was instead a more than competent general. It was Pemberton's further misfortune that his plan dovetailed ideally with Grant's, to the great benefit of the latter.

It is not unreasonable to ask why the South was unable to raise new regiments in late 1862, while the Union, as shown by McClernand, had no difficulty doing so. The answer is that this was yet another effect of the Confederate calamity at Antietam. In addition to the loss of the men and officers of the Army of Northern Virginia, Antietam had cast a pall over the entire Southern cause. The death of the supposedly invincible Lee, and the destruction of his army had crippled recruiting. The effectiveness of the Confederate conscription law was undermined by the hostility of certain Southern governors who, after Antietam, considered the war to be as good as lost, and consequently virtually nullified the effect of the conscription law in their states.

Beginning on November 3, Grant marched south from Grand Junction following the line of the Mississippi Central Railroad, directly on the Confederate position at Holly Springs, Mississippi. Pemberton, seeing no opening to attack the Federals, retreated to a strong position on the Tallahatchie River on November 8. Pemberton was confident that the position could not be carried by a direct assault, and he hoped to draw Grant into attacking him there. Such an attempt, in the Confederate commander's view, would result in a bloody repulse for the Northern army.

Grant was in full agreement with Pemberton's assessment, and had no intention of throwing his men head-on at this obstacle. Instead, he went around it, crossing the Tallahatchie east of the fortifications in the first week of December, and once again forcing the Southerners to retreat, this time to an even stronger defensive line on the Yalobusha River, twenty miles further south.

By early December, three out of the four new divisions of volunteers raised by McClernand had reached Memphis, and were awaiting the arrival of their commanding officer who was personally bringing the fourth and final division. As these men were now in Grant's theatre of operations, and thus theoretically under his command, he proceeded to hijack them for his own campaign before McClernand could arrive to take charge. On December 8, he sent Sherman with one division to Memphis, with orders to take command of the three new divisions. Sherman's force, now designated the XIII Corps and totaling 32,000 men, was embarked on transports in Memphis on December 20, and sent down the Yazoo River. They came ashore at Johnson's Plantation a few miles north of Vicksburg, six days later. Pemberton with the bulk of his army was still at Grenada, more than 170 miles away, blissfully unaware that Grant had stolen a march on him.

Grant's plan had been to engage Pemberton's attention with demonstrations in front of his position on the Yalobusha River, while the real blow was being struck far in his rear in Vicksburg by Sherman's amphibious force. With Pemberton's unwitting cooperation, the plan had worked perfectly.

The defenses along the Chickasaw Bayou north of Vicksburg were so strong that they could be taken by a direct assault only if they were nearly stripped bare of defenders. Through a combination of Pemberton's plan to fight the Federals outside the Vicksburg works, and Grant's end run via the Yazoo, these defenses were indeed almost empty when Sherman arrived on December 26.

The Confederate line ran behind thick tangles of trees alternating with stretches of swamp. The meandering Chickasaw Bayou cut through the Union lines, dividing the attackers into three disconnected pieces, and protecting the center of the Confederate defenses. The defenders were able to shelter behind elaborate earthworks reinforced with abatis (a system of pointed tree-trunks tied together with wire), while their enemies would be obliged to expose themselves as they fought their way through the muck. To make matters even more difficult for the attackers, behind the earthworks were six batteries of artillery sited atop a slight rise (the "Indian Mound"), with interlocking fields of fire which covered all the approaches to the position. In short, it was a defender's dream. At least, it would have been, had it been occupied a sufficient number of men. But for reasons already discussed above, it was not.

In command at Chickasaw Bayou was Brigadier General Stephen D. Lee. He had approximately 2,600 men to defend the three miles of defensive works . As soon as his scouts reported the size of the Union landing force on December 26, Lee called on Major General Martin L. Smith, the overall commander of Vicksburg in Pemberton's absence, to send him reinforcements before he was overwhelmed by ten-to-one odds.

Smith responded to the best of his ability. He immediately shot off a frantic plea for help to Pemberton's headquarters at Grenada on the Yalobusha, and hurried every available man to Lee. However, since Pemberton had already stripped Vicksburg for his mobile force, "every available man" amounted to no more than the pitifully inadequate total of 2,200. So it was that when the battle began the next morning, Lee had fewer than 5,000 men to put in the line at Chickasaw Bayou.

Even with odds of six-to-one on his side, it at first appeared that Sherman's attack might still fail. As at Antietam, although for different reasons, the Union attack went forward piecemeal, rather than as a single, overpowering mass.

Sherman's problems in coordinating his assault were two-fold. First, the battlefield was so cut up by streams, nearly impenetrable woods and mires, that just getting the men in position and headed in the right direction was a considerable challenge, especially for the officers and men of the green divisions fresh from the farms and small towns of Iowa, Indiana and Illinois. Second, the woods were so thick that it was not easy for Sherman to even see enough of the Confederate position to be sure what the right direction for the attack actually was.

Chickasaw Bayou

For these reasons, the initial Union attempts to storm the Rebel position started late, were uncoordinated and were thrown back with heavy losses. Brigadier General George W. Morgan's Third Division began their attack on the Confederate left, which had been scheduled for sunrise, at around 9:30, more than an hour late, because of difficulties getting his men into position. Although the attack was preceded by a strong bombardment from several batteries of artillery, the assaulting column was unable to clear the abatis fronting the Confederate earthworks before the cannons positioned on the Indian Mound behind the line scythed Morgan's men down with volleys of canister. A Union survivor described the attack in a letter home:

"It was a scene taken directly from Hell. On either side, before and behind me, our brave men were swept clear of the embankment by a hailstorm of metal. Arms, legs, heads and other parts of bodies flew into the air, as many of my comrades were literally blown to pieces by case shot and canister. Others lay on the ground, their groans of pain audible even over the deafening clamor of the guns. In no more than twenty minutes time we lost at least 300 men, and as it was plain that the attack was a dismal failure, we were ordered back to our lines..."

(Sgt. Jacob Keller, from: **Tears and Glory: The Official History of the 69th Indiana,** by H. L. Radford.)

The attack by Brigadier General Frederick Steele's Fourth Division on the Confederate right was supposed to have gone in at the same time as that of the Third Division, but due to the difficulty of the terrain, it did not begin until 11:30, which gave Lee time to rush defenders to the other end of the line. Consequently, this attack was repulsed as well, suffering even heavier casualties than the one on the left. By noon, it seemed that a repeat of Antietam was in the works, but with a happier ending for another General Lee.

However, William Tecumseh Sherman was no McClellan, and he did not intend to allow his enemy to thwart him by shuttling troops from one threatened point to another all day. He grimly shook off the loss of over 1,200 men in the morning attacks (he remarked, "We may lose 5,000 men before we take Vicksburg, and we might as well lose them here as anywhere else"), and issued orders to his divisional commanders to launch a renewed assault at four separate points on the Confederate line at exactly 2:00 o'clock.

This new assault began a little raggedly, but by quarter after two there was heavy fighting all along the line. With a prodigious effort, a regiment of Brigadier General A. J. Smith's First Division, the 97th Illinois, captured a section of the Confederate works, losing almost half the regiment, over 450 men, in the process, including the regimental commander, Colonel F. C. Rutherford, who was mortally wounded.

Lieutenant Caleb Hope of the Fourth Mississippi witnessed the desperate fighting that ensued.

"The Yankees pressed forward unmindful of their terrible losses. Every shot by our men seemed to drop another attacker, but for every one that fell, two more would seemingly spring up to replace him. Our fire was so heavy, I still do not understand how any one of them could have survived it. The murky water of the bayou turned pink with their blood, but still they came on, wading chest deep through the muck. I did not see how it was done, but some of them were able to scale the embankment, penetrate the abatis, and jump down amongst us in the entrenchment. There followed a few minutes of indescribable chaos, as muskets discharged inches away from their targets, bayonets severed throats to send blood spraying over friend and foe alike, and clubbed muskets dashed out brains. The combat was accompanied by a hideous noise compounded of curses, shrilly shouted orders, bellows of rage and the shrieks of the wounded and dying, as if a great menagerie of wild beasts had been set upon each other. I was near the forefront of the fighting, and could hardly take a step back, so great the press of men behind me in that narrow space. Suddenly, without warning, I felt the pressure give way, and heard cries of "Fall back, fall back! The Yankees are behind us!" I joined what was left of my platoon in retreat, stumbling to the rear over the prone forms of the dead and the dying..."

(From: **The Face of War: Letters from Confederate Soldiers,** E. A. McHenry, ed.)

This small crack in the dike was quickly followed by the flood. When Lee sent defenders to drive the invaders from the Fourth Mississippi's section, the critical shortage of Rebel soldiers became obvious, as the Federal attacks carried the fortifications elsewhere against the overstretched and outnumbered defenders . Between 2:30 and 3:00, the line was breached in three more places, and the defense on the bayou collapsed. Lee was wounded as he tried to rally the survivors, and was carried from the field on a stretcher. No more than 1,500 of the defenders were able to escape, as the Confederate batteries were overrun, and their own guns turned against them.

By 4:00, Sherman had more than 20,000 men across the bayou at the northern edge of Vicksburg, facing approximately 3,200 men in the Walnut Hills, just north of the town. Secondary defensive positions had been prepared there, although they were not as strong as the one Union troops had already shattered. In addition, practically all of the Confederate artillery had been lost in the earlier fighting.

At 4:30 the Federals attacked all along the line, and in a few minutes the defenders were swamped by overwhelming numbers, the attackers had overrun the last line of defense, and were in the streets of Vicksburg.

By nightfall, the town was in Federal hands, and the Confederate commander, Major General Martin L. Smith, had handed Sherman his sword and surrendered the 2,311 men who were all that remained of the garrison of Vicksburg.

William T. Sherman

Sherman immediately sent a telegram to Washington to announce the victory. "Mr. President, Vicksburg is ours and fairly won. Please allow me to offer you the key to the Mississippi River as a Christmas present."

To Grant he wrote:

"When I crossed the Chickasaw Bayou and saw the strength of the position with my own eyes, I understood how fortunate we were that Pemberton had left only a skeleton force behind in Vicksburg. The siting, design and natural advantages of the fortifications are so great, and the field of operations for attack so limited, I am convinced that 10,000 men, if well supplied with ammunition, could have held that line until Judgment Day against any army in the world. It is solely due to you that the Rebels did not have those men present to put into that line, and we were able to capture Vicksburg. The victory is at least as much yours as much as mine, and you deserve the credit of it."

(From: **Memoirs of William Tecumseh Sherman**)

The loss of Vicksburg was immediately and inevitably followed by the Union occupation of Port Hudson, Louisiana. The town was of no conceivable value to the Confederacy after the fall of Vicksburg and it was abandoned before the Union expedition under McClernand arrived on January 16 (Grant had generously given the political general this booby prize after Sherman's triumph in Vicksburg). From this date onward, the Confederate States of America was bisected, and the end of both the nation and the war to which its birth gave rise were in sight.

William S. Rosecrans

Chapter Four
"This endless retreat"

William S. Rosecrans was a study in contradictions. On the one hand, he seemed to share with George McClellan and the former commander of his army, William Carlos Buell, a military vice which had cost the latter two men their jobs: a reluctance to risk his army in battle, even in the face of orders from his superiors. Having been given the command of the renamed Army of the Cumberland at the beginning of October, he immediately returned to Nashville for a long period of extensive reorganization and refitting, despite urgent orders from Washington to move against Bragg's depleted forces without delay.

Halleck, general-in-chief of the Union armies, wrote to Rosecrans in late October, sending a stern warning :

"The great objects to be kept in view...are: first, to drive the enemy from Kentucky and Middle Tennessee; second, to take and hold East Tennessee, cutting the railroad at Chattanooga, Cleveland or Athens, so as to destroy the connection of the valley of Virginia with Georgia and other Southern states. It is hoped that by prompt and rapid movements...this may be accomplished before the roads become impassible from the winter rains...I need not urge upon you the necessity of giving active employment to your forces. Neither the country nor the government will much longer put up with the inactivity of some of our armies and generals."

(From **General in Chief: The Wartime Correspondence of Henry W. Halleck,** Horace Jenkins, ed.)

Neither the plain warning in this letter nor the fate of his predecessor were able to spur Rosecrans into motion before he felt ready. October, then November came and went, and the preparations of the Army of the Cumberland continued, for a campaign that was beginning to look from Washington as if it would never start.

Rosecrans was popular with his men, who called him "Old Rosie" both because of his name and his prominent nose which owed much of its size and color to the general's fondness for whiskey. The elaborate belt-and-suspenders preliminaries to the campaign were primarily to make sure that his men were well supplied with food, clothing and ammunition for the winter fighting to come, and his soldiers knew it.

Repeated threats of replacement utterly failed to spur Rosecrans into action. When, in early December, Halleck warned that another week of delay might cause the President to remove him, Rosecrans answered, "To threats of removal and the like, I must be permitted to say, I am insensible." He was not satisfied with his command and supply arrangements until December 20, when he finally took his army of out of Nashville, and headed south down the frozen roads of Tennessee.

Now Rosecrans showed the other side of his generalship, a boldness that bordered at times on recklessness, and on occasion crossed that border. Dividing his 68,000 men into three columns under the commands of Major Generals T.L. Crittenden (21,000), George Thomas (23,000) and Alexander McCook (24,000), he advanced on Braxton Bragg's depleted Army of Tennessee, which awaited his approach at the rail and road junction of Murfreesboro. By using three roads his army was able to advance far more rapidly than it would have using only one. However, it also exposed each column to the possibility that it might be attacked and smashed by a superior enemy force before the rest of the army could come to its aid.

When he received word that Rosecrans had left Nashville, Bragg had considered attempting exactly something of this sort, instead of sitting passively behind his field works at Murfreesboro and waiting for the three prongs of the Federal army to converge on him in overwhelming force. He held a council of war on December 21 with his corps commanders, Lt. Generals Leonidas Polk and William Hardee, where he proposed trying to surprise the Federals.

Both Hardee and "Bishop" Polk (the general had been an Episcopalian divine before the war), spoke strongly against the idea. Polk pointed out that their entire force of 26,000 men was only marginally larger than any of Rosecrans's columns, thus making it very unlikely that the Confederates would be able to overwhelm one of the enemy detachments before the remainder of the Union army arrived to crush them. Moreover, Johnston's new Army of Virginia had taken most of Bragg's cavalry, together with his most dynamic cavalry commanders, Nathan Bedford Forrest and John Hunt Morgan, and lacking a superior cavalry force to scout the enemy, create a distraction in his rear and screen the movements of the Confederate army, it would be almost impossible to catch the enemy by surprise, a necessity for the kind of attack Bragg envisioned.

Bragg held another staff meeting on the 23rd, this time to discuss whether the Army of Tennessee should make a stand at Murfreesboro or withdraw before Rosecrans's bigger army, and look for a chance to fight elsewhere under more favorable circumstances. Polk now suddenly suggested a third possibility: that they launch an all-out attack on the Union right under McCook, smash it, then turn on the remaining attacking columns, defeating them in detail. In short, Polk was proposing the very same plan that he had spoken so strongly against two days earlier. Since nothing had changed since then, except that the Union columns were now in a better position to support each other than they had been on the 21st, thus making the odds against success even longer, at first sight this seems so strange as to be inexplicable.

Actually, it was the first step in a carefully planned campaign by Polk aimed, not at the opposing Federal army, but rather at his own superior, Braxton Bragg. Polk's efforts to undermine his commanding officer becomes more understandable when the relationship between Bragg and his subordinates is examined. Unlike his Union adversary, Bragg did not have the common touch that makes a general popular with his men. Nor was he well-liked by the officers serving under him. On the contrary, he had a prickly, disagreeable personality that caused him to be disliked by almost everyone in his command, from his corps commanders down to the riflemen.

BRIG. GEN. BRAXTON BRAGG CSA

Braxton Bragg

Moreover, Polk believed (despite the absence of any evidence to support this belief) that he was far more qualified than Bragg to command the army. He therefore engaged on a campaign to bring about this result.

Thus, when Bragg rejected Polk's proposal, the latter asked whether the commanding general intended to fight at all, or simply continue to retreat, which he said would "undermine the already low morale" in the army. Polk then wrote a letter to Jefferson Davis containing his version of the December 23 staff meeting , wherein he claimed that "The entire army is gradually losing confidence in the current commander," and predicted that the army would soon be rendered unfit for combat if there was no change at the top.

After a stormy session, it was agreed by all that it would be next to hopeless to try to hold the Murfreesboro position. The defensive position was reasonably strong, but both flanks were "in the air', as Bragg lacked sufficient troops to cover them. He therefore faced the threat of being pinned own by Thomas's central column while Crittenden and McCook swept around either end of the line, enveloping his army. So, leaving behind a screen of cavalry under Brigadier General Joe Wheeler to cover the retreat, the Army of Tennessee pulled out of their lines, and headed south down the Nashville Turnpike to a previously prepared defense centered around Tullahoma, the next rail junction south of Murfreesboro.

Rosecrans had been expecting Bragg to give battle at Murfreesboro, and had prepared a battle plan very much like the one Bragg had anticipated, a Cannae-like double envelopment. From this point onward in the campaign, he began to persuade himself that Bragg's army was already beaten and incapable of putting up a fight, and began maneuvering more aggressively than ever.

"They slink away like curs with their tails tucked," Rosecrans wrote to Halleck after he discovered the defenses in front of Murfreesboro had been abandoned without a fight. "We need only to keep up the chase, and their army will fall to pieces."

At the moment, his confidence was fully justified. Still advancing with his army split into three columns, Rosecrans maneuvered skillfully, levering the Confederates out of one position after another with threats to their flanks and rear. After a short, sharp fight at Hoover's Gap on Boxing Day, Thomas's center broke through the undermanned defenses, forcing Bragg to fall all the way back to his main line at Tullahoma. Then, still using his numerical preponderance adeptly, Rosecrans feinted towards Tullahoma with McCook's wing, while sending the bulk of his infantry under Thomas and Crittenden around the Confederate right down the Nashville Turnpike to Manchester, where he threatened to cut Bragg's lifeline, the Nashville and Chattanooga Railroad, at Desherd, ten miles south of Tullahoma.

Alarmed, Bragg once again pulled his army out of their earthworks, and on December 29 sent his weary men in motion to the south. He did not move too soon. Thomas's spearheads entered Desherd just a few hours after Bragg's rear guard had passed through the town.

Over the next two days, both the pursuers and the pursued were slowed by ice storms. Although the weather affected both sides, the thinly clothed and hungry Confederates were hit far harder than the comparatively warmly dressed, well-fed Federals.

"When I joined up at City Hall, an old fellow sitting outside saw me coming out, and told me, "It ain't all fun an' glory, young man. I been there, I know. Most o' the time you'll be too busy tryin' to git enough to eat an' keepin' yer feet dry to worry about how brave you are. If'n yer smart, you'll git yerself a good pair o' boots before you go." I immediately went to the shoemaker, and had a pair of good boots made, for which I paid with the last of my money. As we trudge down frozen Tennessee roads in the middle of nowhere, I am now thankful that I took the old veteran's advice to heart. Many of my comrades lack real footwear of any kind, and suffer tragically during this endless retreat as they march with their feet wrapped in rags, while I am fortunate enough to have dry, reasonably warm feet. The first part of the old soldier's prediction has also been borne out by events. Almost all any of us can think about at present is provisions. No-one in the company, including Captain Ellis, has enjoyed a hot meal in three days. I think this may be true of the entire regiment. Right now, I would cheerfully charge a Yankees earthwork bristling with bayonets, if I could be assured that after the battle a tin of hot beef stew awaited me."

(From **Diary of Private Wallace Caulfield Bitterling**, Roger Newford, editor.)

By New Year's Day, the exhausted Army of Tennessee was in Chattanooga with Rosecrans's Union army bearing down relentlessly on them. Bragg now faced a revolt of his subordinate generals led, naturally, by Polk. On January 1 there was yet another council of war in Bragg's headquarters. This time the contributions of Bragg's division commanders were solicited along with those of Polk and Hardee. The division commanders were the former Presidential candidate Major General John C. Breckinridge, his fellow Major Generals Pat Cleburne, Thomas C. Hindman, Alexander Stewart, Brigadier General William Preston and cavalry commander Brigadier General Joseph Wheeler.

Bragg asked his assembled generals if they could suggest a plan for saving Chattanooga from the oncoming Federals. Instead of producing a battle plan, Polk offered his opinion that the army had lost confidence in its leadership, and that without a change at the top, nothing could be done to reverse the tide of defeat. To Bragg's astonishment, all of his other subordinates but one registered their agreement with Polk, who had pre-arranged the revolt. The latter then presented Bragg with a copy of a letter which he had sent to President Davis in Richmond earlier that day. The letter expressed substantially the same advice Polk had just offered, and bore the signatures of all those present with the exception of Pat Cleburne.

Cleburne, who had not been a party to Polk's conspiracy, walked out of the meeting in disgust. Cleburne did not particularly like Bragg, nor did he think that Bragg was an especially gifted leader, or even a competent one. But he did believe that as the army's commanding officer, Bragg was entitled to the loyalty of the officers serving under him. He later wrote, "It was clear that all of them, Polk, Hardee, Breckinridge and the others, were incapable of putting the interests of the country ahead of their own, and would willingly see Chattanooga fall, if that would rid them of Bragg."

After Cleburne's departure, Bragg, white-faced with rage, told his subordinates that he would promptly write to Richmond for replacements for them, along with authorization to relieve them of duty. Bragg then left the room without another word, went upstairs to his room, and immediately wrote out orders for the Army of Tennessee to pull out of Chattanooga the next day. Then he composed a letter to Jefferson Davis containing his account of this unusual staff meeting.

On this unhappy New Year, the fortunes of the Confederacy in the Western Theatre had hit bottom. Grant's artifice and Sherman's fighters had contrived to take Vicksburg, and thereby cut the infant nation in twain. At the same time, the Army of Tennessee had been driven almost completely out of the state whose name it bore, and appeared to be in the process of disintegrating from internal squabbling without having fought a single major battle in the campaign.

And yet, although no-one could see it, the tides of war, which had been flowing so strongly against the Southern cause since autumn, were about to turn again.

When Jefferson Davis read the letters from Bragg and his subordinate generals, he immediately knew that something would have to be done before the Army of Tennessee collapsed completely. As Davis saw it, there was only one person with the official and moral authority to handle the matter, himself. So, in spite of the impending advance of the Army of the Potomac on Richmond, he felt compelled to leave the capital and go to out Tennessee to meet with Bragg and his generals.

Davis later wrote:

"After I had considered the arguments and actions of the various parties to the dispute, two things became clear. First, although General Bragg was blameless in the matter, and indeed had done everything which could possibly have been expected to save the situation, he would have to be relieved, as he could not count on his junior officers to carry out his commands, and I could not replace them all. Second, I was determined that none of the mutinous officers (for that is what I considered the Generals who had signed the circular letter to be) should be rewarded for their disloyalty. I therefore decided to appoint a new Commander, one who had no prior connection to the internal disputations which had brought the Army of Tennessee to the brink of destruction. I appointed General Bragg to be my military advisor in Richmond, a post which had remained unfilled ever since General Lee had left to take a field command."
(From **The Memoirs of Jefferson Davis**, vol. 2)

Before he named the army's new commander, Davis assembled Bragg's rebellious officers and told them in no uncertain terms what he thought of their behavior. He further warned them that if they were insubordinate to their new commanding officer, he would not merely relieve them of their commands, but would convene courts-martials for them. Polk, who Davis considered to be the ringleader, was relieved on the spot. The dressing down by the President proved to be too much for Breckinridge, who promptly tendered his resignation.

Then he named the new commanding officer of the Army of Tennessee, who he had already summoned, and was on his way to take over. His choice was an unexpected one; a man trusted by neither the public nor his fellow officers, and one whose most recent military achievement had been to lose Vicksburg to Grant and Sherman: Lieutenant General John C. Pemberton.

Ambrose E. Burnside

Chapter Five
"An enemy willing to pay the price in blood"

The very day he took the helm of the Army of the Potomac, Ambrose Burnside began to evolve his plan for a renewed invasion of Virginia. His idea was to avoid the route through Manassas, where the army would be dependent on the vulnerable supply line of the Orange and Alexandria Railroad, a line which would grow more vulnerable with each southward mile. Instead, the army would shift to the east, to enter Virginia via Dumfries and Fredericksburg, and thence on to Richmond. On this route, paralleling the Potomac River, the army's communications could never be cut, as it could always be supplied by water.

Burnside also hoped that his opposite number, General Joseph Johnston would not be expecting this maneuver, so that if he could move his army quickly enough, he might be able to steal a march on the Confederates and be across the Rappahannock River at Fredericksburg and closing on Richmond before Rebels knew what he was about. With any luck at all, he could catch the Johnston's army outside of its prepared fortifications as it hurried back to defend the capital, and with his huge advantage in numbers, destroy it in a single battle.

On December 16, four days after he had taken command, Burnside led the Army of the Potomac out of its bivouac and took it south on what he and his men hoped would be the final campaign of the war. The army had been swollen with new recruits during the long pause following Antietam so that, on December 21, when Burnside arrived in Falmouth, across the Rappahannock from Fredericksburg, he had more than 130,000 men under his command. He divided the army into three Grand Divisions of roughly equal size, and left another 27,000 in reserve at Dumfries, twenty miles to the north. In addition, he had approximately 300 guns in Falmouth, with 100 more in Dumfries.

The first part of operation went off without a hitch, with the vanguard of the Federal Army reaching Falmouth while most the Army of Virginia was still concentrated south of Manassas. Johnston, who had only about 47,000 effectives available to him, had left only a small force of 2,500 men under the command of Brigadier General Sterling Wood in Fredericksburg, as he had considered it unlikely that the Federals would use that route. When he learned that the entire Army of the Potomac had gotten between him and Richmond, Johnston hastily brought his army back to Fredericksburg, sending orders ahead to Wood that he was to hold the town at all hazards or die in the attempt.

Burnside had gotten the jump on Johnston, just as he had hoped, but the next step in the plan called for bridges, and there were no bridges at hand. Trouble with bridges seemed plague Burnside, first at Antietam, and now here at Fredericksburg. He had ordered pontoons to be delivered to Falmouth back on the 15th, but somehow these orders had gone astray. The pontoons, simple, wooden flatboats which could be tied together to form temporary bridges, were not where they were needed in Fredericksburg, and worse still, no one in the entire United States Army was quite sure where they were. Burnside was stymied; the way he saw the matter, without the pontoons, he could not cross the river as he had planned. So, although it meant he would be throwing away the great advantage in position he had gained over Johnston, he could think of nothing to do but sit at Falmouth and wait for the pontoons to arrive. Both here and at Antietam, Ambrose Burnside's lack of mental flexibility would prove costly to his men.

As it happened, the pontoons were only necessary if Burnside intended to cross the Rappahannock directly below Fredericksburg. Only a few miles upstream, on the Federal right, cavalrymen of the 8th Illinois, part of Brigadier General Alfred Pleasanton's Cavalry Division, had discovered a ford which could be comfortably negotiated by foot soldiers. This intelligence was quickly passed on to Major General Edwin Sumner, who commanded the 41,000 men of the Right Grand Division, which was positioned at the ford. Had Burnside ordered Sumner to send his two corps wading across the river to attack Fredericksburg on December 21 or at any time during the next two days, there would have very little Sterling Wood and his undersized brigade could have done about it.

The commanders of the Center and Left Grand Divisions, Major Generals Joseph Hooker and William Franklin, urged Burnside to send Sumner across the ford, and then follow with the rest of the army if the pontoons did not appear within the next 48 hours, but to no avail. Evidently, Burnside feared that if the level of the Rappahannock rose at the wrong time, part of the army might be trapped on the far side of the river, cut off from the rest and annihilated by the Confederates.

If Lee's weakness had been excessive boldness, and McClellan's excessive caution, Burnside's was an excessive reluctance to improvise once an operational plan had been established. He had already demonstrated this mental stolidity at Antietam, and now it returned to bedevil him again. The pontoons did not arrive until New Year's Eve, by which time Joseph E. Johnston and 42,000 soldiers of the Army of Virginia were safely entrenched in the high ground overlooking Fredericksburg.

On December 30, Johnston wrote to Bragg (his relations with Jefferson Davis were still so poor that he avoided communicating directly with the President whenever possible):

"Had the Federal Army crossed the river and continued south immediately, we would have been in a serious, perhaps even critical plight. We would have had no choice but to rush back to give battle somewhere above Richmond, and with the disparity in numbers, such a battle could have had only one outcome. Now that the army is concentrated in strong positions on the heights overlooking Fredericksburg, the situation is considerably more favorable, if not good. I believe this position would be all but impregnable, if we had adequate artillery and a few thousand more men. Lacking these, the heights may be carried, if the enemy is sufficiently determined and willing to pay the price in blood."

(From **Generals of the Confederacy: A Study in Command** by Russell Weigley)

The shortage of artillery complained of by Johnston was one more consequence of the Confederate disaster along Antietam Creek. Lost there, along with everything else, were all of the 246 guns that had gone into action with the Army of Northern Virginia in September, and with the South's inadequate manufacturing capacity, the losses had not yet been made good. Moreover, there now was an additional demand for heavy artillery to bolster the new fortifications around Richmond which were being built up as rapidly as possible in anticipation of a new Union advance. The Tredegar Iron Works, the sole facility for manufacturing guns in the CSA, was obliged to divide its production between the six- and twelve-pounder field guns and howitzers demanded by Johnston on the one hand, and the bigger pieces Bragg desired for the fortifications he was preparing around the capital, and was unable to satisfy the needs of either.

Also lost at Antietam, along with the guns themselves, were the veteran crews who served them. When the battle opened at Fredericksburg, many of

Johnston's artillerymen were fresh-faced recruits who had never seen combat before, as indeed were not a few of the officers commanding them. With inexperienced crews, only 179 six-pounder smoothbores and twelve-pounder brass Napoleons on the heights, and not enough infantry to satisfactorily man the very strong positions, Johnston was aware that it was possible for even a direct assault to take the heights behind Fredericksburg, and if Burnside used his lopsided numerical advantage to maneuver on either flank, the outmanned Confederates would have little choice but to fall back to avoid being trapped.

It was this latter consideration which induced Johnston to order Major General Simon Bolivar Buckner, commanding the Confederate right wing, to shift one of his divisions and 25 guns to Prospect Hill overlooking Hamilton's Crossing, to anchor the extreme right of the defense, on December 30. This move was spotted by Union observers in their balloons and duly reported to headquarters. Burnside interpreted this movement to mean that Johnston was expecting the main attack to come from the Federal left, downstream of Fredericksburg, and concluded that the Confederate center would consequently be weakened and vulnerable.

Burnside had a council of war with his Grand Division commanders on December 30 to hash out the details of the coming battle. He proposed constructing three pontoon bridges downstream of the town, where Franklin was to take his Left Grand Division, consisting of the I Corps (Major General John F. Reynolds) and the VI Corps (Major General William F. Smith) across the river, to turn the right end of Johnston's line at Hamilton's Crossing. To add muscle to this attack, Burnside detached two divisions from Hooker's Center Grand Division and gave them to Franklin, bringing his numbers to about 61,000 including artillery and cavalry.

While Franklin was attacking, Sumner's Right Grand Division, comprised of the II Corps under Major General Darius M. Couch, and the IX Corps commanded by Brigadier General Orlando B. Willcox, was to cross directly below Fredericksburg on three more bridges. Sumner's assignment was to keep Johnston's attention focused on him and away from Franklin, then to attack when Johnston thinned his line in the center in reaction to the pressure on his right flank. To help carry out this assignment, Sumner received four divisions from Hooker's command, swelling his command to 60,000. Thus, each of the attacking Federal columns was nearly fifty percent larger than the entire Army of Virginia.

Burnside assumed that after his men had broken the center of Johnston's line, the shattered Confederate army would be forced to flee willy-nilly. After that, a vigorous pursuit would sweep up the remnants, the Federal army would advance triumphantly to Richmond without opposition, and the war would be as good as over.

At least, this was what Burnside said he intended, as he explained afterwards. His actual written orders on the day of the battle were so ambiguous that what he got was something very different. Franklin understood his part of the battle to be a strong feint, while Sumner's men breached the Confederate center, almost the reverse of what his superior described subsequently. Burnside believed the alleged misunderstanding was a deliberate attempt by Franklin, a friend and supporter of McClellan, to undermine Burnside's position, writing after the battle:

"We had discussed the details of the plan of attack on the heights at a staff meeting on the 30th, and at the end were all in agreement that the Left Grand Division was apply its full strength to turn the southern end of Confederate line behind Richmond Road, and force Johnston to either pull his men away from the center before Sumner's men pressed the attack, or else be enfiladed and destroyed. Yet on the day of the battle, General Franklin contented himself with demonstrations with the bulk of his men, sending only two small divisions forward to engage an enemy who he outnumbered by at least four to one... His [Franklin's] actions can be explained only by his desire to see us defeated, so that his former chief [McClellan] would be restored to command of the Army."

(From **Writ in Letters of Blood: The Story of the Battle of Fredericksburg** by Gregory Erwin)

Franklin's response to this charge was that Burnside's orders on the day of the battle were at considerable variance from what had been discussed the day before. Indeed, there was some justification for this claim. Burnside's written orders did not specify that Franklin was to attack with the entire Left Grand Division, but only that he was "...to send one division at least... to seize the high ground..." behind Hamilton's Crossing. Sumner was given very similar orders: "...to advance west from Fredericksburg with a division or more...to take the heights behind Fredericksburg..." It is, at this point in history, difficult to read Burnside's intentions on that fateful New Year's Eve, but it seems likely that he expected the Confederates to retreat as soon as they saw how badly they were outnumbered by the Union army.

Franklin chose to interpret his rather vague orders literally, and put only two divisions into the attack on his front. Sumner, on the hand, took Burnside's orders to mean that he was to make an all-out effort to storm the Rebel entrenchments on Marye's Heights just behind and overlooking Fredericksburg.

The battle opened just before first light, when Federal engineers began assembling the six pontoon bridges. This part of Burnside's plan went smoothly, with the bridges being completed without opposition. Although Johnston's top subordinates, Buckner and Major General Benjamin F. Cheatham (both of whom had come east from Tennessee in October) urged him to oppose the crossings by stationing troops in Fredericksburg to pick off the Federal engineers while they worked, Johnston declined.

"We are far too thin on the ground as it is; we cannot afford to stretch ourselves any thinner," Johnston told his subordinates. "The idea, gentlemen, is to invite the enemy into the range of our guns, then kill as many of them as necessary, until they either become discouraged or run out of men."

As Union forces assembled on the west bank of the Rappahannock, their artillery, located on Stafford Heights behind Falmouth, began to pound the Confederate center on Marye's Heights, starting at 8:30. This bombardment, which continued for more than an hour, was ineffective for two reasons. First, the defenders were well protected by a sunken road with a four-foot high stone wall that ran along the base of the Heights (this was the beginning of Telegraph Road, which ran parallel to the river here, then curved away to the south and southwest on the Confederate right) . Second, there was a heavy fog over the hills which did not lift until after ten, which effectively obscured the target from the Federal gunners.

When the fog finally cleared, Johnston and his men were afforded a magnificent view of Sumner's Grand Division moving into position on the open fields below. Sumner chose three divisions of the II Corps for the initial attack, 18,000 men altogether. They assembled in long columns spread across the plain between the sunken road which formed the center of the Army of Virginia's position and the town. Packed into the road and behind the stone wall, sheltered from the Federal guns on

Stafford Heights on the far side of the river which continued to pound their positions, were 2,000 of Cheatham's men from Georgia and Mississippi under Brigadier General John K. Jackson. Behind them were another 4,000, and practically all the guns that Johnston had not given to Buckner, 132 of them. These guns were perfectly positioned to cover every square foot the meadow below the sunken road.

As the blue masses formed into columns of attack and began to advance, Johnston asked Cheatham if he was confident that his men could hold the position against the hosts of Federals assembling below. Cheatham replied, "Sir, when those guns open up, a rabbit will not be able to cross that field alive."

Fredericksburg: Assault on Mayre's Heights

First to enter the killing zone was Brigadier General William French's Third Division. French's men came under fire as they approached a canal that ran across their path, two hundred yards west of Fredericksburg. As he had not come forward to see the terrain himself, Sumner was unaware of the existence of this obstacle. The canal could only be crossed at three places over narrow bridges (once again, bridges proved to be Burnside's curse, or rather, a curse for his unfortunate men), and the Confederate batteries were zeroed in on these choke-points. When French's men came over the bridges in narrow columns no more than three abreast, the guns on the hill reaped a deadly harvest. By the time Brigadier General Nathan Kimball's First Brigade was across the canal, and was able to form a line in the shelter of a swale or little "dip" where the direct fire from Confederate guns could not reach them, it had already lost over 100 men to artillery fire.

The subsequent attempt to storm the Confederate position was a bloody nightmare for the Federals. Above the swale was a gently sloping field which was utterly lacking in cover from the defenders' artillery and rifle fire. Kimball's brigade got to within125 yards of the Rebel line before it was shattered by volleys of infantry fire. In just a few minutes 35% of the First Brigade was killed or wounded, including Kimball himself, and the attack ground to a halt.

Next to try were the seven regiments of the Second and Third Brigades under Cols. Oliver H. Palmer and John W. Andrews. A combination of canister from the massed guns and rifle fire from the gray infantry ripped huge gaps in the attacker's lines, killing or wounding more than half of the attacking force before the survivors acknowledged the impossibility of the task.

Captain George F. Hopper of the 10th New York recalled the fighting at Marye's Heights many years later:

"Our men went up the hill bent slightly forward at the waist, as if walking into a strong wind or a hailstorm. But no natural storm has ever consisted of clouds of leaden pellets as this one did. The sound of a Minie ball striking frail human flesh cannot easily be described, but the effects are horrible beyond belief. On either side I heard the peculiar wet thuds of bullets striking my comrades, and saw the results: here, an arm torn almost completely from one man's shoulder, dangling from a few threads of flesh; there, a hole equal in size to a fist suddenly appearing in another's torso amid a spray of crimson, as a ball passes completely through his body and re-emerges from his back; a third clutching his face while blood sprays out from between his fingers, and much more that I will not here describe.

The Rebel line was behind a stone wall which had evidently been improved with additional entrenchments, as there was dirt piled in front of the wall, adding further protection to the defenders. Behind the infantry in the road on the hill above were thousands more, with masses of guns behind, while there was not enough shelter on the field over which we were advancing to conceal a mouse. It was plain to all that the thing could not be done, and that merely to remain upright was an invitation to death, yet somehow our gallant men continued to walk toward the Confederate line. A handful approached within 40 yards of the road before they were laid low. Never before or since have I witnessed such courage in battle, nor such waste of it. Even today, recalling it, I still ask myself what could have kept those men on their feet that day on Marye's Heights.

As the slaughter continued, we heard a chant coming from the hill above us, starting low, and growing gradually louder, until it could be heard plainly over the sounds of the explosions, the malevolent hiss of flying metal and the cries of the wounded: "Sharpsburg, Sharpsburg, Sharpsburg..."
(From **A Knickerbocker at War: Memoirs of George Hopper)**

By noon, it appeared that the Federal attack was not merely a failure, but an unmitigated disaster. But, as Johnston had feared, he simply did not have enough men to hold even so strong a position against a determined attack, even one as poorly conceived and clumsily executed as this one.

Franklin, as we have seen, understood his part in the battle was to provide a diversion while the main attack was being made by Sumner's men. Accordingly, he sent forward only two undersized divisions from I Corps (Major General John F. Reynolds), while continuing to hammer the Confederate right with his guns and making threatening maneuvers with the remainder of his Grand Division. The divisions selected for the attack were the 3rd, commanded by Brigadier General George Meade, and the 2nd, under Brigadier General John Gibbon.

By 11:00, the overwhelming Federal artillery had silenced the Confederate batteries on Prospect Hill, the anchor of the Confederate left, allowing Meade and Gibbon to advance. Gibbon's division of 5,000 moved forward through a small grove of trees, then ran straight into a very strong Confederate position astride an embankment of the Richmond, Fredericksburg and Potomac Railroad held by two brigades from Major General Alexander's division, and was stopped cold. So far, so good.

But the shortage of men meant that some stretches of the seven-mile long defensive line had to be left thinly manned, or in some places, not manned at all. There was a marshy area in front of the Confederate right which General Buckner was told was impassible. Based on this intelligence, he did not assign any troops to cover the 500-yard wide section of the ridge line directly behind the supposedly impassable bog.

As it happened, Buckner had been misinformed. Meade's 4,500 men were not swallowed up by quicksand when they hit the marsh; instead, they slogged through ankle-deep muck, charged the ridge, and found...nothing. There were no Confederate soldiers in evidence other than a few sentries. On either side, Meade's men could see the unprotected ends of the defensive line of the Army of Virginia. To their astonishment, they had walked right into a hole in the middle of the Confederate defensive works.

Meade hastily dispatched a message back to I Corps headquarters, apprising Reynolds of the breach in the enemy line, and asking for reinforcements. At the same time, he ordered his four batteries of divisional artillery, consisting of 16 bronze Napoleons and 8 twelve-pounder howitzers, to join him on the ridge. From here they were in an ideal position to enfilade the Confederate right and center, by blasting the defensive line end-on with deadly effect.

Buckner's only available reserve was a weak second-line brigade under newly promoted Brigadier General A. F. Rudler consisting of 2000 nearly raw recruits from Georgia and North Carolina. These men had received only minimal training before being rushed north to join Johnston's army. This green unit was ordered to take the ridge from Meade's veterans at all costs. The only result of this attack was the slaughter of Rudler's brigade, who were driven off after losing over more than 300 men, among them the C.O., while having absolutely no effect on Meade's men.

By 12:30 Meade had heard nothing from I Corps (it turned out later that the courier had been killed, and Reynolds never received the message), so he took matters into his own hands. He ordered his 1st and 2nd Brigades, along with two regiments of the 3rd, to turn north and attack Marye's Heights from the flank and rear. Although Meade had only 4000 men to put into this attack, they had an effect completely out of proportion to their numbers, and this move decided the outcome of the entire battle.

The defenders panicked as charging blue-coats appeared in and behind their entrenchments, where they had no business being. Makeshift attempts to set up new lines at right angles to the original one were repeatedly outflanked and overrun. Sumner's men, who had been pinned down by the murderous Confederate guns in front of Marye's Heights, immediately felt the slackening of fire from above, and saw the confusion in the enemy ranks. Starting at the regimental level, but moving quickly up the chain of command, new orders to attack were issued, and this time, the attacks went home. By 1:30, Yankees were scaling the embankment and the stone wall, and jumping down into the sunken road in a half-dozen places, shooting the defenders at point-blank range and spearing them with their bayonets.

Johnston was able to salvage most of his army from the defeat. Unlike Lee at Antietam, Johnston had chosen a position from which retreat was possible in the event the battle went against him. He was able to pull part of his unengaged left out of its positions and use it as a rearguard, covering the retreat of his center and right. This rear guard, consisting of Cheatham's division, now under Brigadier General John K. Jackson, held up the Federal pursuit for three hours, until the greater part of the army had made good its escape. Fortunately for Johnston, the Union forces had become almost as disorganized by the suddenness of the victory as the Confederates had by defeat, and it was a long time before Sumner was able to get his men back under control enough to organize a pursuit.

Franklin was slow to recognize what was happening, and he did not order the bulk of his men forward until 4:00, by which time Johnston had withdrawn his Army of Virginia out of the immediate reach of the Union army. The Confederates were allowed to depart unmolested the next day, while the Army of the Potomac rested, licking its wounds.

It is possible, after examining the butcher's bill, to call the Battle of Fredericksburg a tactical victory for the Confederates. The Army of the Potomac lost 12,467 men dead, missing or wounded, while the Army of Virginia suffered only 5,225 casualties. However this fails to take into account the loss of an additional 6,078 Confederates taken prisoner which, when added to the Southern casualties, meant that the total losses of the two sides were very nearly equal.

But what renders any argument that Fredericksburg was not an unmitigated defeat for the South completely untenable is the proportion of losses for the two sides. The Army of the Potomac lost only about 10% of its total force in the battle, whereas the Army of Virginia was reduced by 25%. Moreover, the Union losses were soon made good: two weeks after the battle, replacements had restored the Army of the Potomac to the same strength it had enjoyed on New Year's Eve. Confederate losses, on the other hand, were not. By the end of January, Johnston had still not received replacements for 5000 of the men lost at Fredericksburg.

Even worse, although he had escaped with his army more or less intact, Johnston had been obliged to abandon most of his artillery. The Army of Virginia came away from Fredericksburg with fewer than 50 field pieces, and if men were hard to come by in the Confederacy by January of 1863, guns were becoming scarcer than hen's teeth. The Confederacy had chosen to go to war with an inadequate industrial base against a far more industrially developed opponent, and as the war continued, the cost of this decision became more evident by the day.

There remains the question of why Johnston's battered army was permitted to escape after the battle without any serious attempt at pursuit. Burnside's plan had been successful after all, if not exactly in the way he had anticipated, and he had originally planned a "vigorous pursuit" after the Confederate line had been broken.

It appears that the sight of the II Corps being massacred had unmanned the Union commander. During the height of the heaviest fighting on Marye's Heights, Burnside had to be physically restrained to prevent his crossing the Rappahannock to personally lead a final charge. Burnside was reduced almost to tears by the sight of the carnage across the river, and could not be persuaded to renew the assault, even after the Confederate fortifications had been breached. Hooker vehemently urged him to order an all-out pursuit, but if the Army of the Potomac had not seen enough fighting for the day (indeed, most of it had not fought at all), its commander was mentally fought out.

When he learned that Burnside had allowed Johnson's army to escape, instead of pursuing and destroying it, President Lincoln came close to despair. He wrote to Halleck: "Once again, all the suffering of our brave men is for naught, as their leaders are unable to gather in the fruits of a victory purchased with their blood. How much longer must our poor people continue to endure this terrible war?"

In the end, as Johnston had predicted, the Battle of Fredericksburg was won by a foe willing to pay the price in blood. If the United States continued to be willing to pay that price, the end of the Confederate States of America could not be long delayed.

John C. Pemberton

Chapter Six
"A sudden irruption"

Pemberton's plans for the Army of Tennessee were much like those he had devised for his ill-starred defense of Vicksburg. He intended to keep his smaller force together under his hand, maneuvering it and waiting for the opportunity to pounce on and destroy an isolated detachment of the Union army on a battlefield of his own choosing. The odds against success were long, as he needed many things to break his way before his chance could arise.

First, he required reinforcements, so that he would have enough men available to overwhelm his target before the other Federals could come to its rescue. This requirement was met primarily by taking men from his old Army of the Mississippi and adding a few thousand more scraped from Gulf Coast fortifications (mostly from Mobile) to a few new regiments of draftees. By January 21, Pemberton could count 41,000 effectives in his command, an army that was still considerably smaller than that of his adversary, but one that was now at least capable of defeating a sizable detachment of the Union army, if the opportunity arose. This reinforcement was made possible in part because Grant's Army of the Tennessee had become a victim of its own success by falling prey to divided counsel after the surprisingly easy and rapid conclusion of the Vicksburg campaign.

The politician-soldier John McClernand was dissatisfied the meager share of the glory he had gained from the Vicksburg campaign, and desired an independent command that could generate the kind of newspaper headlines that he had envisioned when he had taken his commission as a Major-General of volunteers. He wrote to President Lincoln, going outside the chain of command and over the heads of his superiors, to ask the Commander-in-Chief to order Grant to give him command of an expedition to capture Fort Hindman (also known as the Arkansas Post) on the Arkansas River. Grant considered this objective to be tangential to the main war effort, and a waste of both time and men, and he had already told McClernand so when his subordinate first raised the idea. Grant wanted to turn his army east into Alabama and Georgia, to take the steel center of Selma and the port of Mobile with Atlanta as the eventual goal. This was the South's largest remaining manufacturing center after Richmond, and the key to the rail system of the southern half of the Confederacy. To Grant's way of thinking, the capture of Atlanta would go a long way toward putting an end to the rebellion, while the capture of Arkansas Post would not bring the Union any closer to victory.

However, McClernand wielded considerable influence in Washington, both with the President and among his colleagues in the House of Representatives. He was a long-time personal friend of Lincoln's, dating back to their years together in Illinois politics, and an influential pro-war Democrat. Because of these purely political considerations, Lincoln reluctantly chose to overrule Grant on this occasion. The President told Halleck to order Grant to give McClernand a corps, and permit him to take it down the Arkansas River to Fort Hindman. Thus, just when the Confederate Army of the Mississippi had been reduced to a force of little more than 10,000 men, the Federal army granted it a stay of execution by turning to chase wild geese west of the Mississippi.

But Pemberton still needed more assistance than this from his enemies. For his plans to succeed, he also required the Union army on in front of him to give him time to gather all his new men together, and to reorganize them into a force that was capable of offensive action. This was provided by Rosecrans' long logistical pause following the occupation of Chattanooga on January 3.

In addition, he had to have at least temporary superiority in cavalry, so that his movements would be shielded from the Union army, while theirs would be known to him. An influx of new cavalry (mostly from the Army of the Mississippi) and the return of Nathan Bedford Forrest from the East, where he had been unable to get along with Johnston, gave him this as well.

Finally, he needed his opponent to do what Grant had not: divide his army in such a way that one portion of it would be vulnerable to an attack, in a place where it could not readily be reinforced by the remainder. In other words, he needed Rosecrans to become overconfident and careless. This final piece fell into place as well.

South of Chattanooga, the terrain is cut up into a series of alternating mountains and valleys running from the northeast to the southwest. It was almost ideal for the kind of ambush Pemberton had in mind. If Rosecrans continued to follow the pattern he had established during the Tullahoma-Chattanooga campaign, Pemberton anticipated that he would divide his army to outflank the Confederate positions, and if he did so carelessly, he could easily expose one of his columns to an ambush in one of these valleys.

Old Rosie was in one of his least cautious moods. He was in fact positively ebullient after his remarkably successful Tullahoma campaign had driven the Confederates out of Chattanooga without a fight. He had persuaded himself that the Army of Tennessee was crumbling, and would fall apart if it was strongly pressed. He wrote to Halleck in Washington:

"The recent influx of deserters from the Confederate camp has convinced me beyond any possible doubt that their soldiers are now without hope of final victory, and are now incapable of any sort of sustained hard fighting. When we proceed from Chattanooga, I intend to harry the Rebels without a pause, until they either stand in place to be annihilated, retreat all the way back to Savannah or the whole of their army melts away."

(From **The Biography of William Rosecrans**, by Hollis Merling)

Rosecrans considered the removal of Bragg to be still more evidence of his enemy's desperation, and he dismissed reports that the Confederate army in front of him had been substantially reinforced. In his battle plan, he urged his subordinates to "press forward in pursuit of the fleeing enemy with the greatest possible rapidity, so as to give him no opportunity to make a stand..." The possibility that Pemberton might not be fleeing did not occur to the Rosecrans. Nor did he seem to harbor any serious doubts about the reliability of information obtained from the deserters, since what they said confirmed what he already believed to be true. The possibility that these "deserters" might have been Confederate plants apparently did not cross his mind. The thought that Pemberton might be laying a trap for him did not enter Rosecrans' darkest dreams.

Rosecrans's plan, as before, was to maneuver three corps of his army, the XIV, XX and XXI, under Major Generals George Thomas, Alexander McCook and Thomas Crittenden respectively, in independent columns, while keeping in reserve 7,500 more under Major General Gordon Granger. While Crittenden with 14,000 men menaced the Confederate positions at the northern ends of Lookout Mountain and Missionary Ridge near Rossville, Thomas would take the 22,000 men of his XIV Corps over the Tennessee River at Bridgeport, then cross Raccoon Mountain and march for the lower end of Missionary Ridge. These two corps would constitute the upper jaw of the trap, and were intended to attract and hold Pemberton's attention. The 14,000 men of McCook's XX Corps would be the lower jaw, striking the flank and rear of the unsuspecting Confederates behind Pigeon Mountain, and grinding them to destruction against Crittenden and Thomas.

One serious problem with this plan was that it depended to a large extent on his opponent being both uninformed about the Federal movements and unsuspecting that anything was happening. In fact, the Confederates were anything but unsuspecting. On the contrary, they were rather better informed about Rosecrans's movements than vice-versa. The Southern cavalry under Forrest had so severely mauled their Northern counterparts (the Cavalry Corps, under Brigadier General Robert B. Mitchell) in a series of vicious skirmishes in the days leading up the battle, that the latter no longer were able to effectively perform their vital scouting function. Rosecrans's notions of exactly where the Confederates were or what they might be doing were mere conjectures. The Union commander had made the mistake warned against by Napoleon of "forming a picture", in other words, basing his plans on what he assumed his enemy was going to do.

The battle began at dawn on January 25, when McCook's men began crossing the Tennessee River at Caperton's Ferry. As they had the longest distance to march, the XX Corps made the earliest start. Almost as soon as the movement began, McCook began to receive reports of suspected large formations of Confederate infantry on Sand Mountain and the southern end of Lookout Mountain, where no Confederates were supposed to be. He passed these reports along to Rosecrans, together with the suggestion that the plan be altered in view this new intelligence, but was told that he faced nothing more than a cavalry screen. Thus, a last chance to avoid disaster was lost.

For the reports of Confederate infantry McCook had received were accurate. Concealed on the far side of Sand Mountain and the lower end of Lookout Mountain was more than half of the Army of Tennessee, 23,000 men under the command of Major General Patrick Cleburne. Had Rosecrans but known it, Pemberton had only about 18,000 men on and behind Missionary Ridge to face 43,000 Federals.

Alexander McCook

The first signs of trouble for McCook's men did not appear until the head of the column entered Winston Gap at the southern end of Lookout Mountain. Lieutenant Colonel Duncan Hall, commander of the 89th Illinois, described what happened:

"I heard a sudden irruption of gunfire to the right, coming from the direction of the wooded slopes on either side of the valley. Almost immediately, the noise grew louder, as more and more rifles joined in, until the sound was almost continuous, and many of my men were killed or wounded by this unseen foe. I immediately ordered the regiment out of column of march and into firing formation, facing towards Lookout Mountain to the east and Sand Mountain to the west, and we began to fight back. The volume of Rebel fire indicated that we were heavily outnumbered, and our regiment as well as the 32nd and 39th Indiana regiments on either side almost immediately began to suffer very heavy casualties. When the concealed Confederate batteries began to fire on us, our losses rapidly became so severe that we had no option but to surrender to avoid the complete destruction of the regiment, as our position was without cover, and we were clearly hopelessly outnumbered. We were not the first to raise the white flag, nor were we the last, but less than an hour after the fighting began, it ceased and most of the 2nd Division was relieved of its weapons, and taken into captivity. It may seem to some that the regiment surrendered without offering a sufficient fight, but after the battle, I could count only 324 men alive and unwounded out of the 645 that went into action that morning, and I challenge anyone who suggests that we were defeated because my men were lacking in courage."

(From: **Into the Jaws of Death: The Battle of Winston Gap** by Douglas S. Freeman)

What happened to the 89th was experienced, with some variation, by most of the XX Corps. McCook himself was wounded in the thigh and taken prisoner, as were the commanders of the 1st and 2nd Divisions, Brigadier Generals Jefferson Davis and Richard Johnson. The commander of the 3rd Division, Brigadier General Philip Sheridan, escaped along with 2600 of his men. The 3rd was the rearmost division, and Cleburne had placed most of his artillery in the middle and southern end of the trap. As his men were not as exposed to the Confederate artillery, Sheridan had time to rally enough of them to break out of the deadly valley back toward Caperton's Ferry. In this he was greatly aided by two batteries of artillery, the 1st Illinois Light Artillery, Battery C, under Captain Mark H. Prescott, and the 1st Missouri Light Artillery, Battery G, commanded by Lieutenant Gustavus Schueler, who covered Sheridan's retreat until all of the gunners were killed or wounded (Prescott and Schueler were posthumously awarded the Medal of Honor) .

As soon as he heard of the ambush at Winston Gap, Rosecrans ordered the XIV Corps to McCook's rescue, but Thomas's men arrived too late to do much more than gather up the wounded Federals that Cleburne's men had left behind. Of live Confederate soldiers, they found none.

In the end, the Battle of Winston Gap proved to be perhaps the most one-sided battle of the war. At a cost of just 1,179 casualties, Pemberton's army had killed, wounded or captured 12,452 Union soldiers. It was an impressive victory, and it was also the last major battle that the Confederacy would win. For, in spite of the near clean sweep of the XX Corps by Cleburne's men, in spite of Rosecrans's hasty retreat back into Chattanooga in the wake of the defeat, the most significant consequence of Winston's Gap was to bring about Rosecrans's replacement by another, more capable Union general.

On January 29, William Rosecrans was relieved of command of the Army of the Cumberland, and replaced by George Thomas. On the same day, President Lincoln now created a new military department embracing the Western Theater from the Mississippi River to the Appalachian Mountains, the Division of the Mississippi. For its commander he named a man who had already inflicted a worse defeat on Pemberton than the latter had on Rosecrans: Major General Ulysses Grant.

George Julian

Chapter Seven
Contraband of War

Although the Civil War did not begin as a war to abolish slavery, it transmuted into one as it progressed. In the few weeks after secession, but before the first shots were fired at Fort Sumter, the abolitionists were in a very bad odor with the Northern public and press. Most Northern whites had little use for blacks. William Lloyd Garrison, Wendell Phillips and their fellow anti-slavery activists received nearly as much blame as Yancey, Ruffin, Rhett and the other Southern fire-eaters for the break-up of the Union. In the view of many angry Northerners, the abolitionists had by their incessant agitation driven the Southern states out of the Union.

But all that changed when the fighting began, and trainloads of coffins containing dead Union soldiers returned home from the battlefields. As early as the beginning of 1862, the war for the preservation of the Union started to look more and more like a war to end slavery, to many members of the ruling Republican Party at least. George Julian of Indiana, an abolitionist and one of the founding fathers of the Republican Party, was one the first Congressmen to call for the abolition of slavery not only on moral grounds, but as a practical a war measure. In a speech to the House of Representatives on January 14, 1862, he said:

"The slaves till the ground, and provide the rebel army with provisions. Of the entire slave population of the South…one million are males, capable of bearing arms. They cannot be neutral. As laborers, if not as soldiers, they will be allies of the rebels or of the Union. Count the slaves on the side of treason, and we are eighteen millions against twelve millions. Count them on the loyal side, and we are twenty-two millions against eight…The rebels use their slaves in building fortifications: shall we not invite them to our lines and employ them in the same business...The rebels employ them as cooks, nurses, teamsters and scouts: shall we decline such services in order to spare slavery?"

Julian even went so far as to suggest using freed slaves as soldiers:

"In the battles of the Revolution, and in the War of 1812, slaves and free men of color fought with a valor unexcelled by white men...in some capacity, military or civil,... they should be used in the necessary and appropriate work of weakening the power of their owners. Under competent military commanders we may possibly be able to subdue the rebels without calling to our aid their slaves; but have we the right to reject it at the expense of prolonging the war and augmenting its calamities?"

(From: **The Congressional Globe**, January 14, 1862)

In promoting the arming and training of freed slaves for combat, Representative Julian was venturing far ahead of where the President was willing to go at the beginning of 1862. Abraham Lincoln had won the Presidency on a platform which promised on one hand to unalterably oppose the extension of slavery beyond where it existed in 1860, but on the other to offer the "peculiar institution" the full protection of the Federal Government where it did exist. Even the outbreak of armed civil rebellion had failed to shift him from this position. As long as he retained hope that the insurrection could be quickly quelled, without resort to what he called "a remorseless, revolutionary struggle" which might scar the nation for generations afterwards, the President refused to bow to pressure from the

Radical abolitionists in his party. In a famous open letter to Horace Greeley, editor of the Radical Republican *New York Tribune*, Lincoln explained the relationship between his war policy and the abolition of slavery:

"As to the policy I "seem to be pursuing" as you say, I have not meant to leave any one in doubt. I would save the Union. I would save it the shortest way under the Constitution. The sooner the national authority can be restored; the nearer the Union will be to "the Union as it was." If there be those who would not save the Union, unless they could at the same time save slavery, I do not agree with them. If there be those who would not save the Union unless they could at the same time destroy slavery, I do not agree with them. My paramount object in this struggle is to save the Union, and is not either to save or to destroy slavery. If I could save the Union without freeing any slave I would do it, and if I could save it by freeing all slaves I would do it; and if I could save it by freeing some and leaving others alone I would also do that. What I do about slavery and the colored race, I do because I believe it helps to save the Union; and what I forbear, I forbear because I don't believe it would help to save the Union. I shall do less whenever I shall believe what I am doing hurts the cause, and I shall do more whenever I shall believe doing more will help the cause…"

(from: **The New York Tribune**, August 22, 1862)

Abraham Lincoln

In this letter, Lincoln made his position absolutely clear: he was fighting the war to preserve the United States, and end the rebellion as quickly as possible. But, it should have been equally clear to the rebellious slave owners that they could not count on his forbearance with regard to slavery forever. The words "...if I could save [the Union] by freeing all the slaves..." ought to have given any reasonably alert Southerner fair warning that the President of the United States was fully prepared to use the tool of abolition, if he felt that this was necessary to win the war.

In fact, it apparently went all but unnoticed in the seceding states. The Emancipation Proclamation was greeted in the Confederacy with outrage and shock, as if they had no idea that Lincoln might take such a step, but the Southerners had no excuse for being surprised.

Above all, what made it all but impossible to stuff the genie of abolition back into its bottle, as Lincoln and many of the more moderate members of his party wished, was the attitude of the bondsmen themselves. The slaves, unsophisticated folk that they were, seemed unable to understand the fine distinction between a war on the persons of slaveholders and a war on the institution of slavery. When the first Federal troops set foot in the territory of the seceding states, slaves living on plantations nearby began to desert their masters and run to the Union lines.

Benjamin Butler

The matter came to a head almost as soon as possible, on the day after Virginia passed its Ordinance of Secession. The commander of the Federal base at Fortress Monroe, Virginia, Major General Benjamin Butler, had been a successful politician and lawyer in Massachusetts before taking a commission in the Union

Army. His legal training proved to be of considerable in his military assignment. In his memoirs , Butler explained what happened when three escaped slaves entered his lines at the tip of the Peninsula in Virginia on May 23, 1861:

"On the day after my arrival at the fort, May 23, three negroes were reported coming in a boat from Sewall's Point, where the enemy was building a battery. Thinking that some information as to that work might be got from them, I had them before me. The negroes said they belonged to Colonel Mallory, who commanded the Virginia troops around Hampton, and that he was now making preparation to take all his negroes to Florida soon, and that not wanting to go away from home they had escaped to the fort. I directed that they should be fed and set at work. On the next day I was notified by an officer in charge of the picket line next Hampton that an officer bearing a flag of truce desired to be admitted to the fort to see me... Accompanied by two gentlemen of my staff, Major Fay and Captain Haggerty, neither now living, I rode out to the picket line and met [Colonel Mallory's representative, Major Carey]... "I am informed," said Major Carey, "that three negroes belonging to Colonel Mallory have escaped within your lines. I am Colonel Mallory's agent and have charge of his property. What do you mean to do with those negroes?" "I intend to hold them," said I. "Do you mean, then, to set aside your constitutional obligation to return them?" "I mean to take Virginia at her word, as declared in the ordinance of secession passed yesterday. I am under no constitutional obligations to a foreign country, which Virginia now claims to be." "But you say we cannot secede,' he answered, 'and so you cannot consistently detain the negroes." "But you say you have seceded, so you cannot consistently claim them. I shall hold these negroes as contraband of war, since they are engaged in the construction of your battery and are claimed as your property. The question is simply whether they shall be used for or against the Government of the United States. Yet, though I greatly need the labor which has providentially come to my hands, if Colonel Mallory will come into the fort and take the oath of allegiance to the United States, he shall have his negroes, and I will endeavor to hire them from him."

Butler went on to explain to his aide the legal principle on which he relied when he refused to return Colonel Mallory's animate property:

"Property of whatever nature, used, or capable of being used for warlike purposes, and especially when being so used, may be captured and held either on sea or on shore as property contraband of war. Whether there may be a property in human beings is a question upon which some of us might doubt, but the rebels cannot take the negative..."
(From: **Autobiography and Personal Reminiscences of Major-General Benjamin F. Butler**)

The contraband concept was neither endorsed nor rejected by Butler's superiors in Washington, but it was thereafter applied by the commanders of many Union armies in the field as a practical way to deal with the issue of escaped slaves. Thus, from the earliest days of the war, whenever Union soldiers penetrated into the Confederacy, from Virginia to Florida, from the Carolinas to Arkansas, they found escaped slaves "voting with their feet", trying to enter their lines, and in many cases, they were put to work for the Union cause.

111

383.   A Group of " Contrabands."
[FOR DESCRIPTION OF THIS VIEW SEE THE OTHER SIDE OF THIS CARD.]

"Contrabands" 1861

This was still a far cry from an official policy of even limited abolition. The status of the contrabands was in a legal limbo. They were not slaves any longer perhaps, but neither were they free. Ironically, what ultimately doomed slavery was the success of the Southern armies on the battlefield. For, if the rebellion had been smashed in 1861 or in early 1862, the process of emancipation might have gone no further than the seizure of contrabands, and it is nearly certain that the institution of Negro slavery would have survived long enough to die a natural death from economic causes.

But, when Lee drove McClellan from the Peninsula in the Seven Days, then followed with a string of victories in northern Virginia, that possibility rapidly disappeared.

After the shock of the First Battle of Manassas, when it became clear in the North that the rebellion was not going to be quickly or easily put down, the policy of confiscating slaves owned by rebels using them to advance the cause of treason against the United State, was embodied in in the first Confiscation Act, which was somewhat reluctantly signed by Lincoln on August 6, 1861. Under this law, slaves forced to work for the Confederate war effort would confiscated and given their freedom after serving as laborers for the Union.

As the war continued, Northern attitudes toward the deprived slaveholders hardened further. Some of the Union generals, such as Buell and Hooker, were still returning runaway slaves to their masters on the basis that they had no proof that the slaves were being used to aid the Confederacy. Others, like Halleck, were simply refusing to allow any slaves inside their lines, while George McClellan showed the political touch that made him so popular with the Radical Republicans by vowing to crush any servile insurrection "with an iron hand". Congress reacted to the policies of these officers in March of 1862, when it passed legislation which forbade army and navy officers from returning fugitive slaves to their owners under any circumstances. But the momentum of abolition was only beginning to build.

Under the Second Confiscation Act, which became law in July, 1862, the President was authorized "to employ as many persons of African descent as he may deem necessary and proper for the suppression of this rebellion, and for this purpose he may organize and use them in such manner as he may judge best for the public welfare", which implied, among other things, that blacks would be permitted to serve in the military.

As we have seen, the Union victory at Antietam in September, 1862 became the occasion for the announcement of the Emancipation Proclamation, although this executive order did not take effect until New Year's Day, 1863. This, like the confiscation policy, was still a wartime measure, but it came closer to universal abolition than anything the Federal government had done previously. Under the Proclamation, all slaves residing in those states which were not under the control of the Federal government as of January 1, 1863, were declared to be free. This executive order, combined with the destruction of Lee and his army at Antietam, sounded the death knell of the rebellion.

The Emancipation Proclamation hurt the Confederacy in three important ways. First, it struck a deadly blow at the Southern economy. For the wealth of the Confederacy was cotton, and the production of cotton depended on the labor of the 2.3 million slaves on the plantations of the Lower South (Georgia, Alabama, Mississippi, Florida, South Carolina, Louisiana and Texas). Once these bondsmen learned that they had been freed by the Federal government, they began to flee from their plantations by the thousand whenever the rumor of Union troops in the vicinity came to their ears.

From the beginning, there were only two ways the South could have defeated the more populous, wealthier and more industrialized North. The first was to win an Austerlitz-type victory, followed by the occupation of Washington or another major Northern city, and force the Union to sue for peace before the southern economy was eviscerated by emancipation and the Union blockade. Any realistic possibility of this happening ended at Antietam with the death of Robert E. Lee and the destruction of the Army of Northern Virginia. By the beginning of 1863, the Confederacy possessed neither an army nor a leader capable of winning the war on the battlefield, and the longer the war continued, the more ruinous were the consequences for the South, as the loss of its pool of slave labor brought its economic system to a grinding halt.

The second great effect of the Emancipation Proclamation was to destroy the South's only other hope of winning its independence: foreign intervention, in particular the intervention of the British Empire. The Confederates had placed an embargo on exports of cotton at the outset of the war, in order to place pressure on Great Britain and its textile mills which depended on Southern cotton. The embargo was intended to mobilize armies of angry, unemployed Englishmen who were thrown out of work by the factory closings in Lancashire, and the equally unhappy owners of those factories who, it was hoped, would force the British government to apply pressure on the Lincoln administration to end the war and reopen the flow of cotton. So as long as the declared goal of the war was reunion rather than the abolition of slavery, there was a reasonable chance that this might happen. But once the war to preserve the Union became a war to end the institution of chattel slavery, the possibility of British intervention came to an end.

When the Civil War broke out in 1860, there was great hostility to slavery in Great Britain. Britain had led the world in the suppression of the Atlantic slave trade, abolishing it within the Empire in 1807, and pressuring other nations to follow (Slavery itself was abolished in the British Empire in 1833.) The Royal Navy enforced the Slave Trade Act vigorously, capturing 1600 slave ships and treating their captains as pirates (that is, by hanging them), freeing 150,000 slaves and eventually, all but putting an end to the trade in the Atlantic.

The anti-slavery movement in Great Britain was spearheaded by a coalition of religious groups who were so successful in promoting their cause that by 1860, slavery had become an anathema to the overwhelming majority of the British public. Indeed, the very factory workers who were most directly affected by the Union blockade and consequent interruption in the supply of Confederate cotton, held public meetings in support of the Union cause, even though many of them faced starvation as a result of the war.

Third, the Emancipation Proclamation created a new source of thousands of fresh recruits for the Federal armies to send against the already smaller Confederacy, by explicitly permitting Negros to join the Federal military, while at the same time depriving the South of the benefits of their labor. In 1860, the total population of the seceding states was 9.1 million, which included 3.5 million slaves, while the population of the nineteen loyal states was 22.3 million. In view of these numbers, it is obvious that if the Confederacy had any hope of survival, it could not permit the armies of its bigger antagonist to add its own residents to their hostile armies, and yet, that is what happened.

In retrospect, it is easy to see that the obvious counter to emancipation would have been to recruit Negros for the Confederate army, with manumission after satisfactory completion of military service being offered as an incentive. However, in spite of the desperate manpower shortage, this was not seriously considered by anyone in power in either the Confederate army or government. This was primarily for ideological reasons. It was widely believed in the South that Negros were by nature so deficient in courage as to be worthless in combat, and so inferior in intelligence that they were incapable of learning the simple skills needed to become soldiers. This belief would have surprised both sides in the Revolutionary War, when thousands of Negros served in the Continental Army and Navy, as well as the British Army and the Royal Navy. In the event, the war ended too soon for them to engage in significant combat, but based on the performance of black soldiers in the United States Army in later wars, there can be little doubt that they would have fought quite as well as their white comrades.

The Civil War was started by a group of slaveholders who believed that the election of Abraham Lincoln would bring about the end of slavery, and with it the destruction of the entire Southern way of life. Ironically, it was primarily the actions of the Confederacy's Founding Fathers that turned this belief into reality.

The mud march

Chapter Eight
"Indescribable chaos"

After the Battle of Fredericksburg, as after Antietam, although for different reasons, the Army of the Potomac paused. However, while McClellan had hesitated to advance south due to his fear of mostly imaginary enemy armies, Burnside was held up by what he perceived as enemies within his own camp.

Before he began the final campaign to take Richmond, Burnside wanted to put his own house in order. He made one important change in his command structure, placing Major General George Meade (Meade was promoted to major general of volunteers as a result of his part in the Battle of Fredericksburg) in command of the Left Grand Division as the replacement for Major General William B. Franklin. Meade's promotion over the heads of so many senior officers was unusual perhaps, but in view of his overall war record, together with his division's vital role in the victory at Fredericksburg, it was understandable.

But Burnside intended the replacement of Franklin to be more than a reward for a deserving officer. It was also meant to be a signal to his subordinates that, however it may have happened, and whatever they thought of his military abilities, until he was relieved, Major General Ambrose E. Burnside was in charge of the Army of the Potomac, and no-one else. Burnside considered Franklin to be insubordinate for his failure to follow orders at Fredericksburg, and suspected that he was disloyally plotting to undermine Burnside's authority in an attempt to bring about the return of George McClellan. In a letter to Halleck written the day after Fredericksburg, he accompanied his report of the battle with the following recommendation:

"General Franklin has worked to create distrust in the minds of his fellow officers by his unjustified criticisms of the actions of his superior and has consistently spoken disparagingly of officers who followed orders which Franklin condemned as foolish. In addition, General Franklin intentionally disobeyed orders at Fredericksburg, and this insubordination nearly led to the loss of the battle. I have relieved him of all responsibilities in this Army, and ordered him to return to Washington. I strongly suggest that he not be given any new command assignment but instead be dismissed from the United States Army, as he is in my opinion, unfit to hold any position of responsibility therein."

(From: **Mr. Lincoln's Generals** by Shelby Foote)

As a result of the victory at Fredericksburg, Burnside had become a popular figure in the North, and as a consequence, his opinions were being given more weight by his superiors in Washington. Nonetheless, while the removal of Franklin was not reversed by the War Department, neither was Burnside's subordinate cashiered, as Halleck and Lincoln were far from convinced that Franklin was unworthy of a command in the army. Instead of being dismissed, Franklin was subsequently reassigned to a corps command in the Western Theater.

By the middle of January, Burnside's plans were complete, and he was prepared to resume the invasion of Virginia. With his huge advantage in numbers, he adopted a plan which disdained strategic subtlety. The Army of the Potomac was still organized in three Grand Divisions of roughly 40,000 men each, with Meade now in command of the Left Grand Division, and Hooker and Sumner still commanding the Center and Right. The Army of the Potomac would advance on the most direct route to the Confederate capital, along the line of the Richmond, Fredericksburg and Potomac Railroad. With a manpower advantage on the order of 3 to 1, Burnside believed that he could simply bludgeon Johnston into submission with his superior numbers. In a letter to Halleck, he wrote:

"If he [Johnston] finds a strong point where he wishes to make a stand, I shall simply use whatever portion of the Army necessary to hold him in place and maneuver the rest around his flanks with the rest. He will be then faced with a choice between retreating or remaining in place to be destroyed when his flanks are turned. If he continues to retreat, he will in the end run out of room, and be forced to either make his stand before Richmond or abandon the city to us."
(From: **One More River to Cross: the Richmond Campaign of 1863** by Bruce Catton)

Johnston was an excellent defensive general, perhaps the best the Confederacy possessed by 1863, but he could see no solution to the problem. He accurately predicted what Burnside would do, but he was at a loss for a way to stop him. "If they are willing to force the issue, and trade life for life in battle, we will soon have nothing left with which to fight," he wrote in a letter to Richmond. "I shall therefore only accept battle in only in those places where our men are strongly protected in prepared fortifications, in hopes of costing the enemy two or three men for each one of ours." He ordered earthworks to be prepared in his rear at several key locations in anticipation of the coming campaign.

On January 15, the Army of the Potomac broke camp, and began its ponderous advance south. Awaiting it in the town of Milford, 20 miles south of Fredericksburg was Johnston and the Army of Virginia. The Confederates had used the time after the battle of

Fredericksburg to good effect, digging substantial earthworks extending for two miles on either side of the railroad where it passed through Milford. The works were occupied by 39,000 men divided into 2 corps, under Major General Benjamin Cheatham and Major General William H.T. Walker (the latter had replaced Simon Bolivar Buckner, who was blamed for the defeat at Fredericksburg).

This position was not as strong as Johnston would have liked, as it was lacking in artillery. As previously noted, the Army of Virginia had lost most of its guns in the hasty retreat from Fredericksburg, and there had not been time to replace them. Johnston had a grand total of 56 guns with inexperienced crews to oppose 257 ten-pounders, twelve pounders and three inch rifles of the Federal artillery served by veterans. Still, if Burnside attacked here, the Confederates would be well protected by field fortifications consisting of elaborate systems of trenches fronted by earthen embankments and reinforced with abatis. Any attempt to take the position by frontal assault would be very costly.

The vanguard of Burnside's army arrived in Milford on the 16th, and began to dig entrenchments facing the Confederate lines, while their artillery set up behind them. Johnston hoped that Burnside might try a direct attack on his lines, and suffer the same kind of losses as he had at Marye's Heights, but he was not to so fortunate this time.

Instead, Burnside used his advantage in men to force Johnston out of his works. He brought the Center and Right Grand Divisions, 83,000 men in all, straight down the line of the Fredericksburg and Richmond Railroad to Milford, while sending the 42,000 men of the Left Grand Division under Meade east and south to outflank the Confederate line east of Bowling Green. When reports of Meade's approach reached Johnston, he immediately issued orders for the army to fall back to the next prepared position, at Hanover Junction where the Richmond, Fredericksburg and Potomac Railroad crossed the North Anna River.

This withdrawal was accomplished successfully, without the loss of a man or gun on January 19. Johnston and his men settled into the new lines on the south bank of the North Anna River, with the Army of the Potomac glaring at them from across the river.

The movement did not look like a success to Jefferson Davis. As the President saw matters, since Johnston had taken command, he had been defeated in a major battle, and had since gone backwards until the Federal army was now less than 30 miles from the capital.

The President did not like Johnston, and had never given him the trust that he had extended to his favorites, such as Bragg, and especially, Robert E. Lee. He had charged Johnston with the defense of Richmond reluctantly, primarily because he had no one else to turn to. The proud and touchy general did nothing to improve relations with his chief. Johnston responded to Davis' coldness by routing all his correspondence to Richmond through Bragg, never communicating with the President directly.

On January 20, Davis summoned Johnston back to the capital for a conference, after reading his account of the withdrawal to Hanover Junction. He told Bragg, "If he [Johnston] has a few more successes like this one, the Yankees will be in Richmond by Washington's Birthday."

As he makes clear in his memoirs, Davis intended to ask the general where and when he intended to fight short of Richmond, and if the answers he received were unsatisfactory, to relieve Johnston and replace him with the only choice at hand, Braxton Bragg. Before he could take this step, Nature took a hand.

Burnside had planned another flanking maneuver to lever the Confederates out of their line on the North Anna, scheduled for January 20. He intended to use Sumner's Right Grand Division (which had been reinforced to 61,000 men) to cross the river east of Hanover Junction at two places. The II Corps (Major General Darius N. Couch) would ford the river at Jericho Mills, 5 miles upstream from Hanover Junction, while the IX Corps (Brigadier General Orlando B. Willcox), would cross on pontoon bridges at nearby Quarles Mill. Once Sumner had engaged the Confederate left, Burnside, with the rest of the army (about 65,000 men), would cross south of Hanover Junction, and Johnston's army would be ground as if between two millstones.

Burnside had great expectations for the success of this operation. He believed that the Johnston would be unprepared for, and that the plan would result in a crushing blow on the Confederate left flank. And even if Sumner did not achieve complete surprise, Burnside was convinced Johnson's men would at a minimum be forced to abandon their fortifications, and would then have no choice but to stage a stand-up finish fight against a Federal Army on the short end of 3-to-1 odds.

The weather, which had been reasonably warm and dry during the first half of January, now suddenly came to the aid of the beleaguered Rebels. At 6 A.M. on January 20, as Sumner's men formed up and left broke camp at Mt. Carmel Church on Telegraph Road, two miles from the ford, the sky began to darken ominously. By the time the last units in the Sumner's Grand Division reached Jericho Mills in the early afternoon, the rain had progressed from a drizzle to a steady downpour, and the red clay of the country roads was turning into muddy slop. The rain, which now was coming in sheets, had turned the usually sedate North Anna into a raging torrent, and the ford was clearly impassible. Nor could the pontoon bridges be used. Even if it was possible to assemble the bridges with the river at flood level (and this was far from certain), the pontoons themselves would first have to be brought to the crossing, and it soon became clear that this really was impossible, because of the effect of the rain on the condition of the roads, as an eyewitness explained:

> "The night's rain had made deplorable havoc with the roads. The nature of the [soil] in this region affords unequalled elements for bad roads. The sand makes the soil pliable, the clay makes it sticky, and the two together form a road out of which, when it rains, the bottom drops, but which at the same time is so tenacious that extrication from its clutch is all but impossible."
>
> (From: the **New York Times**, January 26, 1863)

Although Burnside was forced to accept the impossibility of following through with the plan on the original schedule, he refused to give up. Burnside believed that if the weather improved enough for Sumner's men to cross the North Anna the next day, they would still be able to surprise Johnston and destroy his army.

But the weather did not improve; if anything, it got worse. Over the course of the next three days, neither the rain nor General Burnside relented. In the end, the rain had the victory.

The roads changed from sticky mud into a goo halfway between a solid and a liquid. Wagons, whether loaded or empty, sank into the ooze up to their axles, as did guns and caissons. Nor could they be extricated by horses or mules; the animals too sank in the muck, many vanishing never to be seen again. The men were ordered out to free the trapped wagons and guns, all too often to no avail. The attempt to continue the offensive went beyond the merely impossible to the ludicrous.

"The problem of the soldiers engaged in extricating mules and artillery and [pontoons] was no longer how to keep their shoes from filling with mud, but how to prevent their own disappearance...Imagine a mud-engulfed train of wagons, boats and artillery; the men laughing, shouting and occasionally a mule so undaunted as to join [them]...The men, staggering under the weight of rations, blankets and equipments, formed a funeral-like procession... The disposition to laugh at the long drawn-out wallow of men, mules and mud was general."

(From: **Recollections of a Private** by Warren Lee Goss)

A reporter described the state of the Army of the Potomac after its three day battle with the mud:

"It was a curious sight presented by the army as we rode over the ground, miles in extent, occupied by it. One might fancy some geologic cataclysm had overtaken the world; and that he saw around him the elemental wrecks left by another Deluge. An indescribable chaos of pontoons, wagons and artillery encumbered the road down to the river-supply wagons upset by the roadside-artillery "stalled" in the mud-ammunition trains mired by the way. Horses and mules dropped down dead, exhausted by efforts to move their loads through the hideous medium. One hundred and fifty animals, many of them buried in the liquid muck, were counted in the course of a morning's ride."

(From the **New York Times**, January 26, 1863)

After three days Burnside was forced to acknowledge that the mud had beaten him. He called off the operation on January 24. The so-called "mud march" brought the Union winter campaign to a sudden end.

It also caused a rapid decline in General Burnside's military reputation, which had risen so rapidly after Fredericksburg and the brief campaign that followed. The rank and file of the Army had understood that the victory at Fredericksburg was due far more to luck and the initiative of a division commander than it was to Burnside's generalship, and they had never had great confidence in his military skills. After the fiasco on the North Anna River, doubts about his ability to handle the top command became widespread in the ranks. The army had lost as many men in the mud to exhaustion, pneumonia and related causes as it would have in a major battle, and without a shot being fired. The effect of the mud march on the army's morale was shown by a sudden outbreak in desertions in its immediate aftermath.

Also revived were various anti-Burnside cabals within the Army of the Potomac, which had fallen silent after Fredericksburg and the campaign down to the North Anna River. Two officers from VI Corps, Brigadier Generals John Cochrane and John Newton, both McClellan partisans, took a leave of absence immediately after the mud march, intending to use their political connections (Cochrane had been a Congressman before the war) to have Burnside removed, and Little Mac returned to the Army of the Potomac. They were unable to meet with Cochrane's friends in the legislature (Congress was in recess at the time), but they managed to bring their complaints to the attention of Lincoln and Seward, who agreed to meet them in the White House. In part, Cochrane and Newton were successful, at least to the extent that they were able to plant doubts about Burnside's fitness in the minds of the Secretary of State and the President. What the two generals failed to understand was that Young Napoleon's day was over, never to return. Whatever else might happen, George McClellan was not going to be given another command in the United States Army.

There was another group of subordinates intriguing to bring down Burnside as well. "Fighting Joe" Hooker had gathered around himself a circle of officers who, while they did not long for the return of McClellan, agreed that the direction of the Army of the Potomac was beyond General Burnside's competence, and believed another man would be more suitable for the post. Not surprisingly, the man they had in mind was Hooker himself. Hooker had campaigned for the command at the time of McClellan's relief, after doing what he could to speed along the exit of his former chief, but the prize had eluded his grasp when Burnside was chosen. Ever since, he had taken every available opportunity to promote himself with his superiors in Washington, and to persuade them that Ambrose Burnside was simply not up to the job.

Joseph Hooker

After the mud march, Hooker told a reporter that the army's morale had never been lower. He also opined that unless new leadership at the top could be found, the Union might still lose the war. In the event his meaning was not clear enough, he added that, if it had been competently led, the Army of the Potomac would have already disposed of Johnston's army, and would be at present making its winter camp in Richmond. As the cherry on top of the sundae, Hooker took a page from the departed McClellan's book to add that the country might need to replace the civilian government in Washington with a military dictatorship for the duration before the war could finally be won. From the context, it was not difficult to guess who Hooker thought that dictator should be. The general's remarks came to the ears of the President as he and Secretary Stanton were considering whether a change should be made in the top spot of the Army of the Potomac.

When General Burnside learned of the various plots against him, as he soon did, his response was both prompt and comprehensive, and did him no good at all. He issued General Order 8, which began by relieving Hooker, Newton and Cochrane of their commands, and dismissing them from the Army (although technically, this last was not within his power), then went on to purge the officer corps of the Army of the Potomac of anyone he considered disloyal. Major General William F. ("Baldy") Smith, commanding the VI Corps, one of Smith's division commanders, Brigadier General W.T.H. Brooks, Brigadier General Edward Ferraro, of the IX Corp, and others, all were to be relieved of their posts on the grounds that they had criticized Burnside's handling of the army, or were suspected of doing so. This order was clearly the act of a man in the grip of an unreasoning rage.

It is likely that what drove Burnside to issue General Order 8 was the way his abilities were being openly derided in the ranks after the mud march, and as he could not court-martial or replace all of the men, he focused his wrath on officers who he believed encouraged what he considered disloyalty in the ranks. The main effect of this order was to create doubts in the minds of the Burnside's superiors, not merely as to his fitness for command, but his sanity. Before the end of

January, Lincoln had made up his mind to find a new man to lead his most important army.

The senior corps commander was the veteran Major General Edwin Sumner, and he would have been an easy choice to make, had he been available. Sumner was a steady veteran, who had never joined any of the cliques within the army, and had loyally served the Republic and his superior, whoever he happened to be. However, his poor health and the squabbling of the internal factions in the army prompted him to retire after the aborted crossing of North Anna. He returned home to die of heart failure a few weeks later.

Next in seniority was Major General John Reynolds, commander of the I Corps. Lincoln met him privately at the beginning of February to ask if he would be willing to take command of the Army of the Potomac. Reynolds responded that he would accept only if Lincoln could guarantee that he would be protected from the political pressures that had, in Reynolds opinion, tied the hands of Union commanders thus far in the war. Since the President was not prepared to make any such pledge, Reynolds declined the appointment, choosing to remain a corps commander.

Hooker was next in order of seniority. In his favor was his fine war record. "Fighting Joe" was an outstanding combat commander, having earned his nickname (which was originally the result of a clerical error) at the Battles of Williamsburg, South Mountain and Antietam. On the other hand, Lincoln was reluctant to trust a man who had worked so consistently to undermine his military superiors and who evidently felt no more loyalty toward the civilian government that employed him. To appoint him would give the appearance that the government was rewarding his disloyalty. Perhaps if the war situation had been more desperate Lincoln might have made this choice, but as it appeared by the end of January 1863 that the

Confederacy was on the ropes, he did not feel the need to swallow this bitter pill. Instead of promoting Hooker, the President relieved him, ordering him back to Washington to await reassignment on February 3.

After Hooker came Meade. The Pennsylvanian had risen quickly through the ranks during the war, due to his outstanding performances in several battles, including Second Manassas, where the stand made by his rear guard allowed the Union army to escape destruction, and Antietam, where McClellan selected him to take over I Corps after Hooker was wounded. All this was in addition to his heroics at Fredericksburg, which turned what looked like a blood-soaked defeat into a Union victory. Also in his favor was the fact that Meade was not a member of any of the factions in the officer corps. If he had any criticisms of his superiors, he had kept them to himself. Weighing against Meade was the fact that he was still little known, and that his experience commanding at the corps level was very limited. Entrusting a man who had so recently been only a divisional commander with an army of 130,000 men carried certain risks.

After extensive consultations with Stanton and Halleck, Lincoln made his decision. The President relieved Ambrose Burnside of the command of the Army of the Potomac on February 6, and named George Meade in his place. Thus, like his predecessor, Burnside was sacked after a major battlefield victory, and the Army of the Potomac had its third commander in 47 days.

Ulysses S. Grant

Chapter Nine
"We need only men and ammunition"

With the help of Major General Patrick Cleburne and his men, the incaution of his adversary and a generous helping of good luck, Lieutenant-General John Pemberton had handed the Union cause in the West its worst defeat of the war at Winston Gap, and chased what remained of the Army of the Cumberland back into Chattanooga. Now, he faced the question of what to do with the victory. It was difficult to find a satisfactory answer. It is a measure of the plight of the Confederacy's condition by the beginning of February, 1863, that this victory on the battlefield resulted in such a minuscule long-term advantage.

Pemberton's chief subordinates, led by his brilliant cavalry commander Nathan Bedford Forrest and the aggressive Cleburne, urged him to attack the Federals in Chattanooga and finish them off while they were still demoralized by the recent defeat, and before they could organize the defenses of the city. In spite of the fact that even after its losses at Winston Gap the Federal army still was almost as large as his own, Pemberton gave this idea serious consideration. He went so far as to draw up a plan to attack the Union entrenchments on January 30, then thought better of it after he had taken a long look at position, and at the Federal gun emplacements in particular.

"Any attempt to storm such earthworks without having first suppressed the defending artillery would have inevitably ended in failure, with heavy losses," Pemberton wrote to President Davis, in a February 1 letter explaining why he did not attempt to storm the Chattanooga defenses, "and as we did not possess sufficient artillery of our own to meet this necessary precondition, I could not in good conscience order the attack to proceed."

Forrest, who believed that the Union army in Chattanooga was so demoralized that could be beaten without additional guns, disagreed vehemently. He was so disgusted with Pemberton's decision that he requested and was granted an independent command, and soon left to raid Federal lines of communication in Mississippi.

The remaining option was to keep the Federals bottled up in Chattanooga until starvation forced their surrender. The Army of Tennessee held the high ground overlooking the principal routes into the city: with a few batteries of guns on the heights of Lookout Mountain and Missionary Ridge, they could keep all but a trickle of supplies from reaching the besieged garrison.

Thomas responded by sending away most of his cavalry, so that the few supplies that were able to get in would feed his men rather than the horses, but this was still not enough. By the first week in February, the Army of the Cumberland had gone from half-rations to quarter rations. It looked very much like the garrison was going to have a choice between starvation and surrender. However, the greater Union resources, in the form of men and railroads, once again proved decisive.

While Jefferson Davis did not have a man to spare for Tennessee, Abraham Lincoln had reinforcements and to spare, and the United States had a railroad system that could get them where they were needed. On January 28, over Burnside's protests, three divisions with 21,000 men were taken from the Army of the Potomac, designated XII Corps, and placed under the command of Major General William B. Franklin. In an impressive display of logistics, these men were loaded on trains, and shipped over 1200 miles in 11 days, arriving at the railhead at Bridgeport on February 8. With the addition of these troops, the besieged Federal army now had more than 60,000 men, while their besiegers had only about 40,000.

Grant arrived to take charge in person, and found that Thomas had not been idle. The new commander had reorganized his army, appointing new corps commanders, and prepared a plan to open a supply route into the city. He was only awaiting the advent of sufficient manpower to act on it. When Franklin's men arrived, that condition was met. Grant ordered the plan into effect on February 10.

Thomas' plan involved some elaborate trickery, part of which was floating 4500 men of the XV Corps, Fourth Division (Major General Joseph Reynolds) down the Tennessee River by night for a surprise attack on the Confederate outpost at Brown's Ferry. At the same time, Franklin sent his First and Second Divisions (Brigadier Generals Oliver Howard and Samuel Sturgis) across the river at Kelly's Ferry, then on a night march through Cummings Gap, clearing the road to Brown's Ferry and not incidentally, getting in the rear of the Confederate positions on the northern end of Raccoon Mountain . The combined forces were then to capture the key Confederate outpost on Moccasin Point overlooking the last segment of the route into the city. After that, the Confederates on Raccoon Mountain could be taken from the rear, and the "cracker line" (this was the soldier's name for the supply route) would be secure.

As it turned out, most of the elaborate preparation and planning was unnecessary. Pemberton's forces were so thin on the ground that he had been able to post no more than 1000 men at Moccasin Point. This undersized force was quickly overwhelmed by 6000 Federals. For the same reason, Pemberton had allotted only a single brigade (Brigadier General Marcus Wright) on Raccoon Mountain, which was utterly inadequate to hold this key position against 13,000 of Franklin's men. Wright was forced to hastily pull back to Lookout Mountain to avoid having his whole force enveloped. As it was, he had to abandon two regiments on the northern half of Raccoon

Mountain, where they had been cut off when Franklin's men took Cummings Gap. The Confederate grip on Chattanooga, which had looked so strong, turned out to be surprisingly weak. The opportunity to overrun the Federal army in Chattanooga, if it had ever existed, was now gone for good.

This was just the beginning of the series of misfortunes that would beset the Army of Tennessee in the coming weeks. Their enemies were only going to grow stronger, as more Union armies converged upon Chattanooga.

McClernand had departed for his expedition against Arkansas Post on January 16, and had taken six divisions totaling 32,000 men with him. While the political general was making his bid for military glory, Grant had already begun his next campaign, by moving against Jackson, Mississippi. This key rail junction was held by an undersized corps of 10,000 under Major General Carter Stevenson, which was all that remained of the Army of Mississippi after most of it had been sent to join Pemberton. When Grant advanced on Jackson with 40,000 men, Stevenson had no choice but to retreat, pulling up railway track behind as he did. Union troops occupied Jackson on January 19.

Grant ordered Sherman to pursue Stevenson, and rebuild the rail line across Alabama in preparation for a move east which was to begin as soon as McClernand brought his troops back from Arkansas. Grant did not have long to wait. The garrison of Fort Hindman surrendered on January 23 after a two-day battle, and the expedition was back in Vicksburg five days later. The Army of the Tennessee was therefore consolidated and already on its way in the direction of Chattanooga even before the Battle of Winston Gap.

Sherman's men began to arrive at Chattanooga with on the last day of February, and by March 2, all 18,000 were in the city. The Confederates now faced roughly double their numbers, and the initiative had definitely passed to the Federals. Lacking any better options, Pemberton now had his men entrench in a very strong position centered on the formidable heights of Missionary Ridge and waited to see what his adversary would do.

He was not kept waiting very long. Grant, as in the Vicksburg campaign, did not intend to take Missionary Ridge by frontal assault. Instead, he would use his superior numbers to hold the Confederates in place with one wing while working around their flank with the other. He started on March 8, sending Sherman with 42,000 men of the XV and IX Corps around the south end of Lookout Mountain through Winston Gap, the site of McCook's disaster in January. This time, however, Pemberton did not have anything more than a screening force available to meet the Federals, as Grant had an additional 39,000 men coming out of Chattanooga, apparently intent on attacking Missionary Ridge.

If this was a bluff, Pemberton was in no position to call it. After Forrest's departure, and counting losses from desertions and sickness, he had only 38,000 men altogether, and was now in the same position as the unfortunate Bragg had been during the Tullahoma - Chattanooga campaign. His entire force was smaller than either of the Federal columns, so that even if he could surprise one of them, there was little hope of defeating it before the rest of the enemy army arrived to overwhelm him. "If our whole army attacked [Sherman], we would still not be able to do more than achieve a standoff, and to attempt such a maneuver would be to court the complete destruction of this army." Pemberton wrote later. "Under the circumstances, I saw no choice but to pull out of these lines and withdraw to Dalton to avoid being enveloped."

Pemberton ordered Cleburne, in charge of the Confederate left, to stop Sherman. The latter dispatched a division under Brigadier General St. John Liddell along with a half-dozen batteries to Taylor's Ridge overlooking the road to Dalton. Liddell was ordered to delay the Union advance long enough to allow the rest of the army time to retreat to previously prepared positions on Rocky Face Ridge.

Sherman's XV Corps, who had not seen a Rebel all morning, was taken under fire just after noon, when Liddell's batteries began to shell the First Division just north of the crossroads village of Alpine. The divisional commander, Major General Frederick Steele, hearing the gunfire, rode to the scene and within a few minutes had his leading elements, the First and Second Brigades (Col. Francis Manter and Col. Charles R. Wood) formed into attacking columns and moving toward Rebel positions on the smoke-wreathed Taylor Ridge two miles away. Steele sent word back for his Third Brigade (Brigadier General John M. Thayer) not to follow the other two brigades north from the crossroads, but to continue due east to the town of Somerville, and hit what Steele judged to be the Confederate left flank. He also sent back a messenger to XV Corps, informing Sherman that he had run into resistance.

By the time Sherman arrived at 12:45, a brisk firefight was in progress. Steele's First and Second Brigades had waded through a little stream to the base of Taylor's Ridge, and were exchanging fire with the Liddell's men who were dug in there. The Third Brigade had advanced past Somerville and attempted to overrun the left end of Liddell's position with a bayonet charge. Walthall's Brigade, five regiments of Mississippians, threw them back after vicious hand-to-hand fighting in the trenches. Thayer's brigade lost 450 men killed, wounded or captured before falling back. The defenders lost just over 300.

The pressure on the outnumbered Confederates increased as the afternoon wore on. By two o'clock, the

Second Division (Major General Francis P. Blair,) had reached Alpine, and was adding its weight to the Union push. Sherman had also summoned up all the artillery in reach, and a dozen Federal batteries were working over Taylor's Ridge. Liddell, having carried out his assignment by bringing the Union advance temporarily to a halt, now pulled back to rejoin the main Confederate body which had gotten safely away to new positions on Rocky Face in front of Dalton, ending the Battle of Taylor's Ridge. It would go down as a Union victory, as Sherman's men were left in possession of the field. However, the Confederates got the better of the butcher's bill, suffering 832 casualties as against 1167 for the bluecoats.

Grant and Thomas came over Missionary Ridge with the Army of the Cumberland the next day. They all met in the Chattanooga Academy, a school in the tiny town of La Fayette, Georgia. Grant placed Sherman in overall command of the two field armies which now totaled 83,000, and gave his subordinate his marching orders. "Your objective shall be Pemberton's army. Where it goes, there will you go also. If you can get between him and Atlanta, his army will be destroyed. As he must therefore shield Atlanta, his choices will be limited." Grant, now satisfied that the military situation in Tennessee was well in hand, departed the next day for Mississippi.

Battle of Rocky Face Ridge

After falling back from Missionary Ridge, the Army of Tennessee had entrenched in strong position on Rocky Face Ridge, covering the rail junction at Dalton. Sherman attacked on March 10. He ordered Thomas to use the two corps of the Army of the Cumberland, the IV (Major General Gordon Granger) and the XIV (Major General John M. Palmer) to test the strength of the Confederate positions on Rocky Face and, if in Thomas' judgment they could be carried, to launch an all-out assault. While the Army of the Cumberland was drawing Pemberton's gaze to itself, Sherman was taking the 39,000 men of the XII Corps and the XV Corps (now under Major General Francis Blair, after Sherman's

140

promotion) around the Confederate right, aiming at Dalton in Pemberton's rear.

Thomas sent the First and Second Divisions of IV Corps (Brigadier General Charles Cruft and Major General Phillip Sheridan) to attack the southern end of the ridge at Snake Creek Gap, and the Second Division of XIV Corps (Brigadier General William P. Carlin) the center, while he held the rest of his army back in reserve, in position to reinforce any initial success. The fighting opened at first light with a heavy artillery bombardment, but the attacks by Crufts and Sheridan quickly bogged down when they ran into heavy resistance from Breckinridge's Division (now under Brigadier General Benjamin Helm), and Liddell's Division, backed by strong artillery support, causing Thomas to call off the attack after two hours . Carlin's men had a little better luck, as some of them were able to overrun outlying portions of the rebel trenches, but before Thomas could reinforce them, they were driven out again by the counter-attack of Cleburne's Division (now commanded by Brigadier General Lucius Polk). Thomas, after giving the Confederate earthworks a long look, decided that his men had done enough for the day, and did not order a renewed assault. Altogether, the Army of the Cumberland had lost 1700 men dead, wounded or captured in these diversionary attacks (Confederate total: 1200).

But Thomas' men had managed to fix Pemberton's attention on themselves while Sherman was passing around the Confederate right. Pemberton did not become aware of the threat until late in the morning, by which time Sherman's men were behind his position, astride the line of the Western and Atlantic Railroad, and less than 10 miles north of Dalton. Pemberton reacted by ordering Major General John Forney, in command of his right wing, to fight a rearguard action while Pemberton extracted the army from the jaws of the Federal trap.

Forney in turn, sent his old division, now under Major General Louis Hebert, to throw a roadblock in front of Sherman. Hebert promptly moved his 6200 men into position five miles north of Dalton. At 1:30, XV Corps' Second Division (Brigadier General Morgan L. Smith) ran into Hebert's men. Smith looked over the Confederate position, and decided that it was little more than a screening force. He therefore shifted his division into assault columns, and attacked without further ado, and without waiting for the rest of the Corps to come up.

Smith soon discovered his mistake when his attack withered under heavy fire from Hebert's men. He now reported the situation to his corps commander, Blair, and then to Sherman when he came up. The latter had Blair send Brigadier General Peter J. Osterhaus' First Division around to the right, to see how far the Confederate line extended in that direction. It soon became clear that it did not extend very far. By 3:00, Brigadier General John C. Moore on Hebert's left was reporting that his brigade was under increasing pressure, and he faced the choice of withdrawing or having his flank crumpled by Osterhaus' men.

Hebert understood that it was time to get out or be destroyed. He pulled his men back, yielding ground slowly and reluctantly, holding up the Federal advance for three hours, and giving Pemberton's army time to fall back to new positions further south on the rail line around Tilton. The price for their escape was high, however. Hebert's division was surrounded, and forced to surrender, with only 1,200 of his men eventually making their way back to the Army of Tennessee.

The only positive result of the Battle of Rocky Face for the Confederates was the fact that Sherman had failed to bag the entire Army of Tennessee. In all other respects, it was a disaster. After the near-total loss of Hebert's division was added to the casualties on Rocky Ridge, Pemberton had only 32,000 men left, of which a mere 28,000 were infantry. Sherman, on the other hand, still had more than 82,000 on hand.

The line at Tilton did not last very long. On March 12, Sherman set Thomas' corps on a long swing to the west. This time Pemberton was more alert, and he withdrew without further damage to a previously prepared elaborate system of fortifications at Resaca, three miles south of Tilton, where the Western and Atlantic crossed the Oostanaula River. The earthworks here were also quite strong, but Sherman was not convinced there were enough Confederate soldiers left to hold the four miles of works. He also suspected that the morale of the Army of Tennessee was low after the recent series of defeats, and that it might shatter under a determined attack. If he could break through on the Confederate right and capture the bridge over the Oostanaula, Sherman believed that Pemberton's army, trapped with their backs against the river, would be obliged to surrender.

A heavy fog was clinging to the hills when the battle opened at nine o'clock on March 17, with 120 guns of the Franklin's XII Corps and Blair's XV Corps pounding the Confederate position north of Resaca. At ten, 13,000 men Blair's Corps (Steele's First Division and Third Division, under Brigadier General James Tuttle) alongside Franklin's Third Division (Brigadier General Daniel Sickles), stormed the formidable-looking trenches, in part to test the numbers and determination of the defenders there, but more importantly to draw Pemberton's gaze and his reserves thither.

This attack, like the one Thomas had attempted on Rocky Face, was repulsed, but with much heavier Union losses. While Thomas had not renewed the attacks after the first try convinced him it could not succeed, Sherman ordered two more attempts before conceding that the position was too strong to carry by direct assault. A captain in Steele's division described the third and last attempt:

> "To give a true description of this terrible charge is simply impossible. We stumbled forward over the still forms of men who had fallen in the first two attacks through a dreadful volcano of lead and iron that even worse than that which greeted us previously. Our loss was very heavy and to no visible purpose."
> Captain Frederick S. Washburn, 9th Iowa
> (From **Death in the Morning: Infantry Tactics in the Civil War** by H. R. Rossman)

Sherman's attempts to break the Confederate right cost his men 3400 casualties in just ninety minutes, while his enemies lost only 800 men. On the third attempt, a few Federal soldiers managed to get into the trenches before the defenders, Missourians of Major General John F. Bowen's Division, killed or captured them, but this was enough to cause Pemberton to shift men from his left to shore up the right against the possibility of a renewed and more successful effort. Thus the Confederate left was thinned of men just when the main Union attack was launched there, a little after noon.

George H. Thomas

Thomas had been given this assignment. He had 32,000 men available for a frontal assault on the section of the defensive line in the hills overlooking Camp Creek, just outside Resaca. If his men could capture this part of the trench system, they would be athwart the railroad that was the Army of Tennessee's lifeline, and would hold the bridge over the Oostanaula, cutting off the only practicable line of retreat.

Cleburne, in command on the Confederate left, instantly saw the danger. He called for Pemberton to return the men he had taken, and assembled all the artillery he could lay hands on behind his men. He had only 5,000 men to hold a mile of trenches against Thomas with six times that number. They were not enough.

Battle of Resaca

First to clear the abatis and ditch fronting the Confederate works were men from the First Division (Brigadier General Absalom Baird), Third Brigade (Brigadier General John H. King), three regiments of US Army Regulars. Although they lost over a third of their number before they were able to scale the parapets and come to grips with their enemies, King's men disregarded their terrible losses, continuing to attack with reckless bravery, some firing down at the defenders at point-blank range, others leaping in among Cleburne's men, dueling with bayonets or swinging their rifles like clubs in the close quarters combat. A desperate effort by Brigadier General Daniel C. Govan's brigade finally ejected the Federals, after a fight in which both brigade commanders were killed.

The extreme left of Pemberton's line, where the trench ended at the bluffs overlooking the Oostanaula, was the closest part of the line to the Resaca bridge, and thus the most vital point of the defense. Here the line was anchored by a strong log and earth stockade fronted by a palisade of sharpened sticks and a ditch, called Fort Cleburne. Indiana and Illinois regiments of the Fourth Division's First and Second Brigades (Colonel John T. Wilder and Brigadier General Milton S. Robinson) stormed Fort Cleburne and took it, in spite of ferocious resistance by three batteries of guns under Major Felix H. Robinson, which continued to blast the attackers with canister at close range until all the men working the guns were killed or wounded. By 12:45 Robinson's men had captured the last line of trenches, and the way to the bridge was momentarily open. They were driven back temporarily after being enfiladed by the guns Cleburne had assembled and a charge led by Cleburne personally, which recaptured the last line of trenches. Cleburne was wounded in the fighting, and was out of action when a final Union surge broke completely through the position at 1:30. Heedless of the many corpses from both armies which covered this small patch of ground, soldiers of the Third Division (Brigadier General John M. Brannan), Second and Third Brigade (Colonels John T. Croxton and Ferdinand Van Derveer) overran the batteries which had temporarily stopped the Fourth Division, and captured the section of trench guarding the bridge for good. Brushing aside a few cavalrymen who stood in their way, some of Brannan's men rushed down the hill into Resaca to occupy the bridge, while the others attacked the now-open end of the Confederate line.

The fog was so thick that the Third Division's breakthrough was not immediately apparent to Thomas, and a messenger sent back by Brannan failed to reach him immediately. This gave Pemberton time to organize a final counterattack to recapture the bridge before Union reinforcements reached it. All he had available was Liddell's Division, which had been battered in the hard fight at Taylor's Ridge just a few days before, and now mustered only 3600 effectives. At 2:30, they charged the Union forces holding the Atlantic and Western Bridge, trying to reopen their army's escape route.

Although the attack was pressed home with great courage (Liddell's men took over 1000 casualties), the task was more than mortal flesh could achieve. Liddell's attack was stopped before it reached the bridge, and there was neither time nor men available to organize another before Thomas sent two more divisions into Resaca, and the vital bridge was gone for good.

Fighting continued to sputter on until early evening, but the issue had already been decided. At six o'clock, Pemberton sent out a messenger with white flag to ask for Sherman's terms. With the surrender of the Army of Tennessee on March 17, the armed forces of Confederate States of America east of the Mississippi River consisted for all practical purposes of roughly 10,000 infantrymen of the Army of Mississippi, 2,500 cavalry under Nathan Bedford Forrest, and the Army of Virginia, with perhaps 40,000.

***

Grant left Tennessee on March 9, confident that the situation in north Georgia was now well in hand. He had urgent business elsewhere, specifically with XIII Corps, under Major General John McClernand. After Sherman had taken his men to Chattanooga, Grant had assigned

McClernand to pursue and crush Major General Carter Stevenson's rump Army of Mississippi. Stevenson had retreated down the line of the Mobile and Ohio Railroad after the Union occupation of the rail junction at Meridian on February 3. After reaching Meridian, McClernand, with more than 30,000 men, had been unable to go much further.

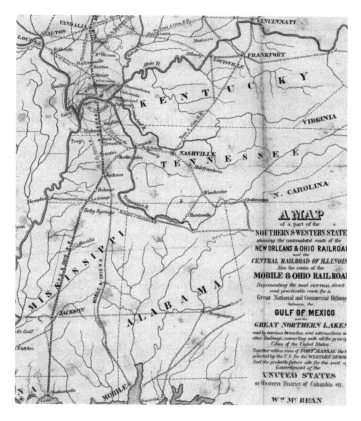

Railroad map of Mississippi and Alabama

This was largely due to the activities of Buell's old nemesis, Nathan Bedford Forrest, who had been released by Pemberton at his own request, and given an independent command. He now returned with his raiders to bring misery to the men attempting to keep McClernand's supply lines open. Operating with no more than 2,500 men at any one time, Forrest's attacks on Union trains, depots and track in Mississippi brought McClernand to a standstill. So much of his force had been detailed to chase Forrest, guard the supply line and repair the damage done by the raids, that he had advanced only as far as Quittman, just 25 miles south of Meridian, by the beginning of March. McClernand, whose eye was always on his public image, told reporters that his lack of progress was due to Grant's failure to provide him with sufficient cavalry support to stop Forrest. This was at considerable variance from the truth. In fact, Grant had sent the Army of the Tennessee's Cavalry Brigade (Col. Cyrus Bussey) with 2200 horse soldiers to join the XIII Corps, as the besieged Army of the Cumberland in Chattanooga did not have sufficient fodder for its own animals. With the addition of Bussey's men, McClernand had more than 4,000 cavalry at his disposal, which was significantly more than Forrest's whole force.

Grant descended on Quittman on March 11, and relieved McClernand of command of the XIII Corps, citing his statements to the press as the reason. He was replaced by Major General James B. McPherson, a protégé of both Grant and Sherman. When the campaign began, it became clear that McPherson would command the re-designated Army of the Eastern Gulf in name only, as Grant himself would be running the show.

McClernand was offered the meaningless position of second in command to Grant for the Department of Mississippi, a trick that had been played on Grant himself by Halleck after the Battle of Shiloh. Rather than accepting this nugatory assignment, McClernand asked to be sent back to Washington for re-assignment, where he hoped his political connections would provide him with another field command. Grant did not hesitate to approve this request.

Grant now proposed a daring solution to the supply problems caused by Confederate cavalry raids, raids which had crippled Buell's Tennessee campaign in 1862, and had now brought ten times their own number to a halt in Mississippi. He would cut loose from his supply line, and live off the land.

"The enemy before us is demoralized, beaten and badly outnumbered. We need only men and ammunition to defeat him, as the country will supply all our other needs." Grant telegraphed to Halleck. In a week, he had gathered 100 wagons full of ammunition, and another 1000 empty ones for his foragers. He started south from Quittman along the line of the Mobile and Ohio on March 18. Stevenson, still outnumbered by 3 to 1, had little choice but to fall back.

Grant's men swept wide into the countryside on either flank, gathering cattle, pigs and chickens from the wealthy plantations of southern Mississippi. Plantation owners, those few were not away with the Confederate army, fled before them, as did the overseers. The effect on the plantations, many of which were run by women in the absence of their menfolk, was drastic. An eyewitness wrote in her diary:

"I saw a band of blue-coats coming over the hill...like demons, they rush in! To my smoke-house, my dairy, pantry, kitchen, and cellar, like famished wolves they come, breaking locks and whatever is in their way. The thousand pounds of meat in my smoke-house is gone in a twinkling, my flour, my meat, my lard, butter, eggs, pickles of various kinds - both in vinegar and brine - wine, jars, and jugs are all gone. My eighteen fat turkeys, my hens, chickens, and fowls, my young pigs, are shot down in my yard and hunted as if they were rebels themselves... Grant himself and a greater portion of his army passed my house that day. All day, as the sad moments rolled on, were they passing not only in front of my house, but from behind; they tore down my garden palings, made a road through my back-yard and lot field, driving their stock and riding through, tearing down my fences and desolating my home."

(From **A Woman's Wartime Journal** by Dolly Summer Lunt)

On the other hand, the slaves fled in the opposite direction, towards the Yankee invaders and freedom, carrying with them everything they owned. Soon, the Federal army was being trailed by a ragged mass of newly emancipated slaves. Some of these camp followers Grant put to work as porters, mule skinners, cooks and launderers. The healthiest young men were recruited for service in the new Negro regiments being formed pursuant to the Emancipation Proclamation.

The phenomenon of a former field hand now in uniform, with a rifle on his shoulder, marching past the planation where he had been a slave just a few weeks earlier, spelled the final doom for the institution of slavery, no matter what ultimately happened on the battlefield. Abolitionist writer Frederick Douglass recognized the significance of the black regiments more clearly than even the United States government. Speaking to a recruiting rally in Philadelphia, Douglass said, "Once let the black man get upon his person the brass letters, U.S., let him get an eagle on his button, and a musket on his shoulder and bullets in his pocket, there is no power on earth that can deny that he has earned the right to citizenship."

Stevenson set up a new line 27 miles south of Quittman in a system of works outside the town of Waynesboro. He did not expect to stop the Federal advance there, but only to delay it long enough to complete and occupy the elaborate system of fortifications being prepared behind him at Mobile. He fully expected Grant to use his advantage in numbers to flank him out of the line at Waynesboro. He was therefore pleasantly surprised when the Union general did not attempt to maneuver, but stopped in front of Waynesboro and began to entrench, as if in preparation for a siege operation.

In fact, Grant had no intention of attacking at Waynesboro, and was perfectly content to allow the Confederate army to sit there in its trenches. Indeed, this fit perfectly with arrangements Grant had made before he had broken camp at Quittman.

Hundreds of slaves had been taken from local cotton plantations (much against the wishes of their owners) and employed digging the earthworks around Mobile. Runaways from among them reported that the garrison had been stripped of men to provide reinforcements for Pemberton, and Mobile was woefully unprepared for an attack. All that remained to defend the Confederacy's last major port on the Gulf were 1100 men in Fort Morgan and Fort Gaines guarding the entrance to the bay (a third fort, Fort Powell was still under construction), and a few regiments of half-trained militia. This inadequate force was under the command of Brigadier General Richard L. Page. The Confederate Navy was planning to block the entrance to Mobile Bay with naval mines, but these would not be ready for several months.

Rear Admiral David Farragut was in New Orleans with his Gulf Blockading Squadron, and had been available for operations in the Gulf since the fall of Vicksburg at the end of December. At Grant's suggestion, he was now given orders from Washington to take Mobile while Grant kept the Confederate Army of Mississippi busy, before the city's the land or sea fortifications were ready. For his landing force, Farragut was assigned Brigadier General Thomas Sherman's Second Division of XIX Corps (Major General Nathaniel Banks).

Farragut's expeditionary force arrived on station in the Mississippi Sound at the head of Mobile Bay on the night of March 22. The Union squadron consisted of a half-dozen wooden-hulled steam sloops of war, all veterans of the Battle of New Orleans, with Farragut's flag flying in *Hartford*, escorting a dozen transports carrying Sherman's 7200 men. As he had at New Orleans, Farragut decided to run the Confederate batteries by night, trusting darkness and speed to foil the 10-inch Columbiad smoothbores and 7- and 8-inch rifled cannons in the forts. *Hartford* and *Brooklyn* led the transports into Mobile Bay, while the other Federal warships screened them and exchanged fire with the Confederate batteries until the rest of the expedition was clear. This turned out to be easier than expected, because the forts had been designed to cover the seaward approaches, and the guns could not be traversed to bear on ships once they penetrated into the lower bay.

The only Union casualties were aboard the steam frigate *Richmond*, which was struck by a shell that ruptured her steam lines and killed 6 sailors. The remainder of the force passed safely into Mobile Bay, out of range of the forts and was ready to begin landing Sherman's men in Mobile at dawn. At nine o'clock, Farragut called on the Confederate commander, Brigadier General Page to surrender. With fewer than 2000 militiamen to defend the city against over 7000 Union regulars backed by the big guns on Farragut's ships, he had little choice but to do so. Mobile was in Union hands, and the Army of Mississippi suddenly found itself trapped between two Union armies, with no good place to retreat. Grant's uncharacteristic spell of lethargy at Waynesboro was explained.

It was also emphatically ended. The day after the fall of Mobile, Grant got his army into motion again, sending the Ninth Division (Brigadier General Peter Osterhaus) on a wide swing around the Confederate right. Stevenson, deprived of his planned refuge in Mobile, fell back again. With no clear goal in mind, he retreated in the only direction available: east into Alabama, abandoning Mississippi to the Yankees. By then he also knew that Pemberton had surrendered, and that his army would almost certainly soon be facing Sherman's men coming from north Georgia to join Grant, giving his enemies well over 100,000 men against his dwindling force. In addition, the Confederate supply system in Alabama had completely broken down after Pemberton's surrender after Sherman's men had confiscated all the locomotives of the Atlantic and Western Railroad within reach and rode down to occupy Atlanta, which capitulated without a fight on March 21. Without the prospect of any kind of resupply, and with his little army melting away by the day, Stevenson yielded his 7,500 men to Grant on March 24. Appropriately enough, the surrender of the last active Rebel army west of the Appalachians took place in Montgomery, Alabama, birthplace of the CSA.

West of the Appalachian Mountains and east of the Mississippi, apart from Forrest's cavalry raiders (Forrest would soon see the hopelessness of the situation, disband his army and surrender to Federals in Jackson a few days later), the Confederate States of America was a thing of the past.

George Gordon Meade

Chapter Ten
"Let the thing be pressed"

In January, the weather had intervened to save Joseph Johnston's Army of Virginia from its enemies. Eventually though, the ground would dry, the roads would harden, and the Union army, now under George Meade, would resume its march south. And when it did, Confederate prospects would be no brighter than they had been before the rains had brought the Northerners to a halt.

Johnston used the pause to improve the system of entrenchments around Hanover Junction. He made repeated requests for reinforcements and additional artillery, warning Richmond that without them he lacked the means to defend the capital. As neither additional men nor guns were available, these requests were denied.

Meade took advantage of the layover to reorganize his army. He scrapped Burnside's Grand Divisions, finding them unwieldy in practice, and leaving the existing corps commanders in place. He did like the idea of the Cavalry Division (Brigadier General Alfred Pleasanton), another of Burnside's innovations, which combined several smaller cavalry units into single division. He liked it so much in fact, that he increased its size by adding the cavalry brigade (Brigadier General George Bayard) from Smith's VI Corps. This enhanced Cavalry Division gave Meade a potential striking force of 11,000 mounted men capable of independent operations deep in the Confederate rear areas. By contrast, the Army of Virginia's Cavalry Corps (Major General Frank C. Armstrong) at end of February, 1863, consisted of two undersized divisions with a total of no more than 6,500 men, the remnants of Nathan Bedford Forrest's corps which had been brought east after Antietam. The Confederates were still, man-for-man, superior horsemen, but that superiority was not enough to overcome twice their number of foes.

By the beginning of the fourth week of March, the roads had hardened enough for Meade to resume the march on Richmond. He began on March 22 by sending the Cavalry Division across the ford at Jericho Mills, five miles upstream from Hanover Junction, with orders to raid the Confederate rear areas all the way down to Richmond, destroy depots, burn bridges, pull up track, generally disrupt Johnston's supply line between Hanover Junction and the North Anna and provide information on the state of Richmond's defenses.

746.   A Canvas Pontoon Bridge.
[FOR DESCRIPTION OF THIS VIEW SEE THE OTHER SIDE OF THIS CARD.]

Pontoon bridge over the North Anna river

The next day, Meade put his main body in motion. The right wing, consisting of II Corps (Major General Darius Crouch), IX Corps (Brigadier General Orlando B. Willcox)and III Corps (Brigadier General George Stoneman), 49,000 men altogether, with Crouch in overall command, was given the task of holding Johnston's attention by threatening the Richmond and Fredericksburg Railroad Bridge and the Chesterfield Bridge directly in front of Hanover Junction. While Crouch kept Johnston in place, Meade took the 66,000 men of the left wing (V Corps under Major General Daniel Butterfield, I Corps under Major General John Reynolds, and VI Corps under Major General William Smith), over the river 5 miles downstream on pontoon bridges.

Johnston had his men sheltered in a system of earthwork fortifications at Hanover Junction along a railroad embankment overlooking the North Anna, with artillery (what little he had of it) covering the two bridges. This position was very nearly as strong as the one on Marye's Heights where Burnside had nearly wrecked Sumner's corps. This was where Johnston expected and hoped the main Union assault would come. To encourage this expectation, Meade had left most of the Federal artillery with Crouch, ordering it to shell the Confederate lines as if in preparation for an assault.

Meade's plan succeeded in making Johnston hesitate long enough to allow his men to cross the river downstream unopposed. By nine o'clock, the entire force was across the river and marching up the line of the Virginia Central Railroad, threatening to take the Confederates in the flank. Johnston, recognizing his peril, ordered Major General William Walker, in command of his right wing, to form a new line facing Meade's forces, by deploying Walker's old division (now under Brigadier General Matthew C. Ector) on either side of the railway embankment.

Just after noon, the leading elements of Meade's men ran into Walker's new line. The first assault was launched by the First Division (Brigadier General Griffin) of V Corps. Taking advantage of the protection afforded by a slight elevation, 10 regiments of Colonel Claudius C. Wilson's Georgians and Colonel William Hugh Young's dismounted Texas cavalry stopped Griffin's men in their tracks. When he arrived on the scene, Meade told Butterfield to call off this uncoordinated attack, wait for the rest of his corps to come up, and then send all 18,000 men in at once. He ordered Reynolds to take I Corps around to the left of Walker's line, probing for the flank and rear of the Confederate position.

Johnston was now truly alarmed. If Reynolds' men reached the line of the Richmond and Fredericksburg Railroad behind his army, they would be between the Army of Virginia and Richmond, the road to the capital would be would be open to the invaders, and Johnston's army would be cut off. He ordered Walker to promptly attack the Federal column, and stop it at all costs, while Johnston extricated the rest of the army from what was rapidly becoming a trap.

He also ordered his artillery, which was already sited on the Richmond and Fredericksburg Bridge to spend a few salvos attempting to destroy the bridge to slow down the Union pursuit. This would be the last chance to use what remained of his field pieces, as they would have to be abandoned in the hasty retreat, if Johnston was going to be able to save any of his army.

Walker selected the divisions commanded by Major General Alexander Stewart and Brigadier General William Preston for the attack. Preston and Stewart assembled their men in a thickly wooded ridge that overlooked the road I Corps was using without being detected. By the time they were in place, the First Division (Brigadier General Abner Doubleday) at the head of the Federal column had already passed their position. At 2:30 10,000 Confederates let loose a hair-raising rebel yell, and rushed down from the hillside into the middle of the startled Yankees. Although they were outnumbered 2-to-1 by Reynolds' corps, the Confederates achieved tactical surprise, and were able at first able to throw the Federal column into disarray. Two brigades of Meade's old command, the Third Division, were routed, and for a short time it appeared that the entire division was going to be swept away by the attack. Then the Pennsylvanians of the First Brigade (Colonel William McCandless) rallied, hurriedly forming in a horseshoe around two batteries of guns on a thickly wooded little knob, and stopping the Confederate charge in some of the most ferocious infighting of the war.

> "Rebel infantrymen, seeming to come from all directions, climbed up and fired into the faces of our men; some grappling hand-to-hand with the defenders, while others dueled with bayonet thrusts between the close-set trees; continuous musketry fire cut down saplings, and snatched every leaf from the branches... the artillery took advantage of every opening in our ranks to fire case shot and canister into the gray mass... Shrieks of wounded men, explosions, curses, howls of anger all mixed together, created an indescribable clamor. From time to time, the fighting was swallowed up in clouds of smoke, only to emerge again, as desperate as before ..."
> Captain William C. Talley, 1st Pennsylvania Reserves
> (From: **Eyewitness to War,** Charles McCall, ed.)

Before the Rebel attackers could overrun this knot of resistance, the First Division came to the rescue of McCandless' men. As soon as he became aware of what was happening behind his division, Doubleday turned his men around and hastily formed them into columns of four. They fired one volley, then charged into the flank of Stewart's division with fixed bayonets. The tables were suddenly turned, as now it was the Southerners who were taken by surprise. The Confederate counter-attack swirled away in confusion, leaving behind 2,300 men dead and wounded. Union losses were comparable.

Although they were finally driven off, Walker's men did succeed in temporarily stalling the Federal advance. By the time Reynolds had gotten his units disentangled and moving in the same direction again, Johnston had been able to pull his men out of the earthworks in front of Hanover Junction, and escape encirclement, covered by a stubborn rear-guard action by Ector's division. The Battle of Hanover Junction cost the Confederates 2754 casualties, while the Union lost 3112 men, and once again, the Confederate army was able to slip away.

This time, however, there was a fundamental difference. By the time Johnston had gotten his army clear, a retreat directly south along the Richmond and Fredericksburg was no longer feasible, as elements of the Union I Corps were already on the rail line. He was therefore obliged to retreat to the southwest, and by nightfall, when the Army of Virginia finally halted after crossing the South Anna River on the Ground Squirrel Bridge, 10 miles southwest of Hanover Junction, it was further away from Richmond than was the Army of the Potomac. From here, Johnston could no longer interpose his army between the Yankees and the capital.

The Confederate army now faced a grim prospect. They would have either have to fight a running battle south against more than twice their numbers to reach the fortifications around Richmond, 25 miles away, before Meade's army did, or else continue southwest before turning back toward the capital, hoping to shake off their pursuers and enter Richmond from the west. Neither option offered much hope.

If the Johnston attempted the former, it was reasonably certain that his army, now reduced after Hanover Junction to fewer than 40,000 men, and with virtually no artillery, would be crushed by Meade in the open field before it ever reached Richmond. On the other hand, if Johnston chose the longer road, there was little doubt that capital of the Confederacy would have fallen before he could get there.

Johnston dispatched a message to Davis, telling him that he could no longer protect Richmond, and advising him that if the government did not flee the city immediately, it risked being taken by the Yankees.

Immediately after the battle, Meade sent a telegram to Lincoln describing the victory at Hanover Junction, and adding "If the thing is pressed, I believe we can be in Richmond tomorrow. " Lincoln's prompt response was, "By all means, let the thing be pressed."

That night, Meade received good news from his Cavalry Division. They had ridden all the way to the outskirts of Richmond, intercepting and destroying a supply train on its way to Johnston and burning several bridges, then had run into Armstrong's Cavalry Corps six miles outside Richmond, where the Fredericksburg and Richmond Railroad passed through Cedar Swamp. Pleasanton's men had prevailed after a three hour fight, and had driven the Confederate cavalry off. More important than this skirmish was the fact some of Pleasanton's men had gotten a good look at the city's defenses from close range. They reported that the works were far from complete, and moreover, appeared to have very few men in them. Pleasanton gratuitously added that his division would have been able to carry the fortifications unaided, but as this was outside the scope of his orders, he had refrained from making the attempt.

With this intelligence in hand, Meade issued new orders for the next day. Couch was to take the three corps of the right wing, which had not fought at all that day, and were therefore fresh, the remaining 20 miles to Richmond, and if the cavalry reports proved to be accurate, capture the city before the Confederates could find men to put into the earthworks. Meade himself would follow Johnston's army with the other three corps, and attempt to force a showdown with the Confederates outside their protective fortifications. He ordered Pleasanton to attack Johnston's lines of communication and prevent his army from being resupplied from Richmond.

Davis had put Braxton Bragg in charge of Richmond's defenses in February, but had unable to give him with more than a handful of soldiers to man them. Bragg's army consisted of mainly of 4,500 regulars who had been taken from the defense of Goldsboro in North Carolina, leaving the vital rail line they had been guarding dangerously vulnerable. All he had in addition to this small force were some only partially-trained militia units composed of men either too young or too old for the draft. Bragg believed the latter units had little or no military value.

Bragg and Davis had an urgent meeting to discuss Johnston's note on the night of March 23. After a strenuous debate, the general persuaded a reluctant President Davis that the city was indefensible, and that the government must be evacuated at once. Messengers were immediately sent out to members of the Confederate Congress and cabinet secretaries, with some being called out of their beds after midnight.

By the next morning, rumors of the approaching Federal army and the impending fall of the city were all over Richmond, fueling panic and rioting. The streets thronged with the overloaded wagons and carriages of residents fleeing the doomed city with whatever they could carry. Criminals who had broken out of jail when their guards absconded, were joined by like-minded citizens in taking advantage of the opportunities created by the collapse of civil government, breaking into shops and warehouses, stealing food, clothing and anything else that came to hand (especially liquor), and celebrating wildly, in some cases by setting fires which soon spread unchecked through the city. A witness recalled:

"...the fiery billows rolling on from house to house, from block to block, from square to square, unopposed by the stupefied, bewildered crowd...Through that terrible day, all through the succeeding night, the smoke of [Richmond's] torment went up to heaven. Strange, weird, the scenes of that night, the clouds of smoke hanging like a funeral pall above the ruins, the crowd of woe-begone, houseless, homeless creatures wandering through the streets... "
(From: **The Atlantic Monthly**, June 1865)

Richmond after the fire

When the first Federal soldiers reached the outskirts of Richmond late in the afternoon on March 24, they were greeted by dense clouds of smoke rising from the stricken city. With civil order gone, and without any realistic hope of successfully defending the city, Bragg had ordered his men to pull out, and Meade's men met no resistance when they entered Richmond.

Stoneman, whose III Corps was the first on the scene, ordered his men to clear civilians from the streets, and start fighting the fires. They were helped more of Crouch's men, who joined in as they arrived, and the Union soldiers were able to extinguish the fire by the next morning, saving what was left of the city. The bulk of the Crouch's 60,000 men passed through or around Richmond and headed west along the James to re-join Meade in the pursuit of the Army of Virginia.

The Confederate flag was hauled down from atop the Capitol on Shockoe Hill by Johnston de Peyster, a young Lieutenant on the II Corps staff, who replaced it with a Union flag. He wrote to his mother, " Arriving at the capitol, I sprang from my horse, first unbuckling the Stars and Stripes, a large flag I had on the front of my saddle. With Captain Langdon, chief of artillery, I rushed up to the roof. Together we hoisted the first large flag over Richmond, and on the peak of the roof drank to its success." For this feat, the 18-year-old de Peyster received a brevet promotion to Lieutenant Colonel.

Meade, with the larger part of the Army of the Potomac, spent the day relentlessly running his quarry to ground. Johnston had been forced to abandon his wagon train at Hanover Junction, and his men had no food beyond the scanty provisions they had been able to carry away with them. The state of the ammunition supply was much the same. Many of Walker's men, who had been involved in heavy fighting the day before, were running low or almost out of ammunition, and the train that was supposed to bring them more rounds for their rifles had been waylaid by Federal cavalry and never arrived.

In his March 23 note to Richmond, Johnston had described his army's desperate predicament, and asked for a supply train to be sent to a rendezvous with the army at Lorraine, a small town located 10 miles west of Richmond on the north bank of the James. During the night of March 23rd and into the early morning hours of the 24th, with a final effort amid the chaos attending the fall of Richmond and the collapse of the Confederate government, the Commissary Department managed to put together a wagon train and load it with provisions and ammunition for Johnston's army. It left for Lorraine late in the morning, which proved to be too late to do Johnston's men any good.

After defeating the Confederate cavalry at Cedar Swamp, Pleasanton's men were unopposed as they brought destruction to the track, locomotives, rolling stock of the railroads that ran west from Richmond, and anything else moving west from the city. Johnston's re-supply column did not escape their attention. It was overtaken by the Cavalry Division's First Brigade (Brigadier General John Farnsworth) on the Rock Hill Plank Road, five miles west of Richmond, and went no further.

So it was that when Johnston arrived in Lorraine, he almost immediately discovered that no new supplies of either provisions or ammunition would be forthcoming. Behind him, his men, discouraged, weary and hungry, began to lose hope and fall by the wayside and be scooped up by the advancing Yankees. Meade's soldiers, on the other hand, sensed that their enemies were on their last legs, and were consequently energized. By three o'clock, Doubleday's men, in the van of the Federal column, had overtaken the rear of the Confederate army, forcing Matthew Ector's division, which had seen hard fighting the day before, to turn and fight .

With only 4,000 effectives, the beleaguered Southerners were soon facing the 8,500 men of Doubleday's oversized division. There ensued a fierce, but brief battle, before Ector's men began to surrender, a few here and there at first, then whole regiments at a time. Possibly they were discouraged by the sight of smoke rising from Richmond as it burned in the distance, or it may have been the unrelenting pursuit by the well-fed, confident bluecoats, but whatever the reason, the Army of Virginia was beginning to come apart.

The little town of Lorraine backed on the deep, broad James River. The nearest bridge, 4 miles east, was already in the hands of Federal troops. The next closest bridge was 8 miles to the west. With the Federal Army blocking the way east and north and the James at their backs, this was the only possible escape route. Johnston therefore prepared orders for the army to march west along the river at sunrise.

Units of Meade's army continued to arrive, even after the sun had set, taking up their places in the dim afterglow that precedes nightfall. When the stars came out, Johnston's men looked out at a semicircle composed of thousands of campfires extending from the banks of the James ahead of them, to the west, to the river's edge behind. They were trapped.

Joseph E. Johnston

In the morning, Johnston consulted with his corps commanders, Walker and Cheatham, to see if they thought it worthwhile to attempt a breakout, or whether they should simply surrender. Neither of Johnston's subordinates believed their men were capable of launching an effective assault. Walker, however, insisted that his men were still able to repulse any Union attack, and stated his belief that talk of surrender was premature

.

Johnston later wrote:

"I did not agree. I compared the military forces... They having one hundred twenty thousand, we, thirty thousand...It was clear to me under the circumstances, it would be the greatest of human crimes to continue... Having neither money nor credit nor arms but those in the hands of our soldiers, nor ammunition but that in their cartridge boxes, there can be no question of going on. I said that I would ask Meade for terms."

(From: **Narrative of Military Operations** by Joseph E. Johnston)

The signing of the surrender took place in the office of the Lorraine postmaster's house. Meade offered generous terms: Johnston's men were obliged to surrender their arms and were then immediately paroled after swearing to never again take up arms against the United States. In return, Meade promised that neither officers nor men would be imprisoned or charged with treason as long as they honored the terms of their oaths. He further allowed the men to take home their mules and horses, and the officers to retain their side-arms. When Johnston told him that many of his men were starving, Meade ordered 100,000 rations be distributed to them.

The news of Johnston's surrender soon reached the remaining Confederate armies in the field. On March 27,

Armstrong surrendered the remnants of the Cavalry Corps. Bragg and P.T.G. Beauregard, the latter commanding the military district encompassing North and South Carolina, surrendered three days later. By April Fool's Day, all organized resistance to the United States government east of the Mississippi had ended. The Trans-Mississippi District, consisting of Texas and Arkansas, which had been cut off from the rest of the Confederacy since the fall of Vicksburg in December, surrendered on April 10, after General Kirby Smith, who commanded the military district, confirmed the news from the east. The Civil War was over.

For Jefferson Davis, the war never truly ended. As he fled west from Richmond, the members of his government travelling with him gradually abandoned the aimless journey. A company of Federal cavalry who had been assigned to capture Davis finally caught up with the fugitive President near Asheville, North Carolina on April 24, nearly a month after Johnston's surrender. He refused to acknowledge the fact that the country he had helped to create no longer existed. "So long as the love of liberty lives in the heart of one loyal Southerner, [the CSA] will never die," he wrote in his memoirs. He never forgave his generals for surrendering, and he went to his deathbed believing that the South could have won the war had it not been betrayed by its military leaders.

The American Civil War lasted two years. It cost the two sides the lives of 285,000 young men (Union 155,000, Confederate 130,000), of whom 125,000 died in combat, with the remaining two-thirds succumbing to disease due to exposure, poor sanitation, wound infection and other by-products of military life. In addition, another 160,000 suffered wounds, many resulting in permanent disability. This was the price for the abolition of African slavery in the United States as measured in blood. It was a terrible price, but if it had not been paid the South might have never escaped from its dependence on slave labor and the resulting moral and economic dilemmas created by that dependence.

Afterword

The American Civil War is by far the single most popular historical subject in the United States . Consequently, there is an overwhelming amount of material available for anyone interested in the American Civil War. To give just one example, more than one hundred books on the Battle of Gettysburg alone are published *every year* (http://www.h-net.org/reviews/showrev. php?id=9583). The Civil War was, moreover, the subject of an 11 1/2 hour documentary film by Ken Burns which was seen by 40 million people when it was initially broadcast, making it the most watched documentary in the history of television. So, it may well be that anyone interested enough in the subject to purchase an alternate history of the Civil War would be reasonably familiar with the facts of the non-alternate (or actual) war.

On the other hand, it is unrealistic to expect every reader to be intimately familiar with the details of this vast, complicated subject, so I still see some value in providing an abbreviated history of the war, if only to refresh faded memories. The fact that this book begins in 1862 with the Antietam campaign, while the war itself starts in 1861, is reason enough to justify the condensed history of the conflict presented below.

1860

The states of South Carolina, Mississippi, Alabama, Florida, Louisiana and Texas secede from the Union over a period of 7 weeks starting in December. The triggering event is the election of Republican Abraham Lincoln to the Presidency of the United States. Delegates from the seceding states meet in Montgomery, Alabama in February, where they adopt a new constitution and select Mississippi Senator Jefferson Davis to be President of a new nation, the Confederate States of

America. Soldiers of the new nation seize Federal property in various places, including several military installations and armories, but no immediate clash of arms takes place.

1861

On April 12, Confederate batteries under the command of General P.G.T. Beauregard shell Fort Sumter in Charleston, South Carolina, forcing its garrison to surrender. Northern public opinion, which has up to this point has been unenthusiastic about forcibly putting down the rebellion, is electrified by this attack on Federal troops. Almost immediately, Lincoln is inundated by demands from politicians, publishers and regular citizens urging him to take some strong action in the emergency. He responds on April 15, issuing an executive order to arm and train 75,000 militiamen to suppress the rebellion and calling Congress into a special session. The President's declaration of his intention to use force to preserve the Federal government proves to be too stern a test for the loyalty of the states of Virginia, North Carolina, Arkansas and Tennessee, all of whom join the rebellion over the course of the next several weeks. Virginia's importance to the infant nation is acknowledged when the capital is moved from Montgomery to Richmond in May. The four slave states of the upper South (Delaware, Maryland, Kentucky and Missouri) remain in the Union. All but Delaware are occupied and fought over by the armies of the combatants during the course of the war. By the end of May, the CSA is as large as it will ever be, comprising 11 states with a total population of 9 million (including 3.5 million slaves). The new nation now prepares for war against 19 loyal states with an aggregate population of 20 million. On July 21, the first major battle of the war is fought, along the Bull Run Creek near Manassas Junction, Virginia, between half-trained armies of volunteers. It results in a Union defeat. The Battle of Bull Run serves notice to the North that the war will be neither short nor bloodless. George McClellan is appointed by Lincoln to the command of the most important Federal army, the Army of the Potomac, on July 27. In November, when the ancient Winfield Scott retires, McClellan is appointed general-in-chief of the Union armies, although he has done nothing but train his men since taking the reins of the Army of the Potomac.

1862

In the West, the Union is victorious in the early battles. Ulysses S. Grant occupies a nearly undefended Fort Henry on the Tennessee River on February 6, 1862, then surrounds and captures Fort Donelson after a sharp fight on February 16, taking 12,000 men of the Confederate garrison prisoner. The victories open the Cumberland and Tennessee Rivers to Union gunboats, obliging the Confederates to abandon Nashville to the Federals on February 23. In March, McClellan, who is under increasing pressure from Lincoln to take the army he has been training for 8 months into combat, begins his invasion of Virginia. He uses the Union control of the waterways to shift his army of 120,000 men to Fort Monroe on Chesapeake Bay at the tip of the Virginia Peninsula, thus bypassing the Confederate earthworks at Manassas Junction and Centerville which block the direct route from Washington to Richmond. Confederate General Joseph Johnston counters by withdrawing his army to new positions on the Peninsula between McClellan and Richmond. On April 4, McClellan begins his advance toward Richmond, 60 miles away. Although his army outnumbers the Confederate Army facing him by more than two to one, McClellan moves slowly, and does not reach the vicinity of Richmond until the end of May. Johnston, believing that loss of Richmond is inevitable if his 60,000 man army remains on the defensive, attacks on May 31. The ensuing Battle of Seven Pines is bloody, costing the two armies a total of 11,000 casualties, but tactically inconclusive. The most important result is the wounding of Johnston, which knocks him out of action and leads to the appointment of Robert E. Lee in his place. Elsewhere, while the Army of the Potomac has been inching along the Peninsula, Thomas "Stonewall" Jackson has been campaigning in the Shenandoah Valley, trying to prevent another Federal Army from descending on Richmond from the west. Between March 23 and June 9, Jackson, with 17,000 men, fights six battles, defeats three Union armies totaling 52,000, then returns to join Lee in time for the Seven Days Battles. McClellan is so shaken by Seven Pines that his slow advance now comes to a complete halt. On June 24, the Army of the Potomac is only six miles from Richmond: it will not get as close again for nearly 3 years. Lee, with 85,000 men after Jackson joins him, now plans not merely to save Richmond, but to destroy the Federal army, which now numbers 105,000. In a series of six battles from June 25 to July 1, he fails, but does succeed in lifting the threat to the Confederate capital. Lee loses 20,000 men in the Seven Days, while McClellan's army suffers16,000 casualties. In the Western Theater, a Confederate army of 44,000 men surprises Grant's slightly larger Union army on April 6, in the Battle of Shiloh (Pittsburg Landing). After 2 days of heavy fighting, the Confederates are defeated. Shiloh is the bloodiest battle of the war to date, resulting in 13,000 Federal casualties and 11,000 Confederate, a record that will soon be broken. Although Shiloh is a Union victory, Grant's reputation suffers as a result of unfavorable newspaper coverage, and he is put on the shelf for four months, and consequently nearly resigns from the army. On April 25, New Orleans, the largest city in the Confederacy, falls to a fleet of warships under Flag Officer David Farragut.

The Second Battle of Manassas (Second Bull Run) is fought on August 29-30. Once again the outcome is a Southern victory, when Lee and Jackson combine to maul John Pope's Army of Virginia. The battle costs Lee's army 8,500 men, while the Union army suffers 10,000 dead and wounded, and is forced to retreat. In August, Braxton Bragg and Kirby Smith lead 40,000 Confederates north to invade Union-occupied Kentucky. They run into the slightly larger Union Army of the Ohio under Don Carlos Buell in the bloody but indecisive Battle of Perryville on October 8. While the Yankees suffer the greater losses (4,200 vs. 3,400), after the battle, Smith and Bragg retreat back into Tennessee. Buell's failure to pursue the retreating enemy causes Lincoln to replace him with William Rosecrans. In September, Lee leads the Army of Northern Virginia on an invasion of Maryland which results in a collision with the Army of the Potomac at Antietam on September 17. McClellan with 75,000 men attacks Lee's army of 50,000 in its positions on the heights overlooking Antietam Creek. The ensuing battle produces the bloodiest single day of the war, with the armies suffering a total of 22,000 casualties (Union 12,000, Confederate 10,000). For all the bloodshed, the Battle of Antietam (Sharpsburg) is indecisive. Afterwards however, Lee is obliged to abandon his invasion of Maryland, and withdraw his battered army to Virginia. This makes Antietam enough of a victory for Lincoln to announce the Emancipation Proclamation on September 22, an executive order freeing all slaves in the states which are still in rebellion as of January 1. With this, the underlying cause of the war comes to the forefront, and the issue becomes the preservation or destruction, not just of the Union, but of the institution of slavery. McClellan, after repeatedly refusing to obey orders to pursue Lee's army, is relieved on November 7, and replaced by Ambrose Burnside. At the Battle of

Fredericksburg (December 11-15) which follows, Burnside's plan results in one of the most one-sided defeats of the war, when more than 4,000 Union soldiers are shot in two hours while attempting to storm Marye's Heights. In all, Fredericksburg costs the North 12,500 men, while the South loses fewer than half that number. After his next plan results in the fiasco of the "mud march", Burnside is relieved, and replaced by Joseph Hooker. On December 26, Grant's first attempt to take Vicksburg is smashed at the Battle of Chickasaw Bayou, when Sherman's attempt to storm the defenses is repulsed with a loss of over 1700 men (Confederate losses: 200). The Vicksburg campaign will continue for another six months.

1863

In his greatest victory, Lee defeats Hooker and the Army of the Potomac at Chancellorsville (May 1-4), dividing his army of 60,000 repeatedly in the presence of a Federal army of more than 130,000. The Union casualties are 17,000, Confederate 13,000. In the course of the battle Jackson, Lee's most valuable subordinate, is wounded and loses his arm. He dies of an infection resulting from the surgery on May 10. In June, Lee invades the North again, taking his army into central Pennsylvania through the Shenandoah Valley. Hooker resigns after a dispute with his superiors in Washington, and is replaced on June 28 by George Meade. The two armies clash again at Gettysburg on July 1. In the 3-day battle that follows, the Army of Northern Virginia is defeated and is forced to retreat back to Virginia. Gettysburg is the bloodiest battle of the war, with each side losing 23,000 men. In Mississippi, on July 4, Grant concludes a campaign that began in December, when John Pemberton surrenders Vicksburg and its 29,000 man garrison to him after a 66 day siege. The loss of this city effectively cuts the Confederacy in two. In

Tennessee, William Rosecrans' army is defeated at Chickamauga (September 19-20), avoiding complete destruction largely due to the efforts of George Thomas, who wins the nickname "the Rock of Chickamauga". The Confederate Army of Tennessee under Braxton Bragg suffers the greater losses, more than 18,000 compared the Union's 16,000, but the Federal army is forced to retreat into Chattanooga on the Tennessee River, where it is besieged. In November, at the Battle of Chattanooga (November 23-25), the reinforced Union army under Grant breaks the siege, defeats Bragg's army and drives it from the hills overlooking the Tennessee River.

1864

Grant is promoted to Lieutenant General on March 3, the first to reach that rank in the U.S. Army since George Washington, and is given command of all Federal armies. He goes east to take over the Army of the Potomac, leaving Sherman in charge in the west. In May Grant leads the Army of the Potomac into Virginia on the Wilderness Campaign (May4- June 24), fighting 3 major battles (the Wilderness, Spotsylvania Courthouse and Cold Harbor) and many lesser ones. By July, the Army of Northern Virginia is forced to fall back into fortifications covering Petersburg and Richmond. In the heaviest sustained fighting of the war, the Wilderness Campaign costs the Union 55,000 men dead and wounded, while the Confederates lose 33,000. In the west, over the course of 3 months, Sherman with 110,000 men, employs a series of flanking maneuvers to drive Joseph Johnston's army of 60,000 from the hills near Chattanooga back to the outskirts of Atlanta, over 100 miles away, without fighting a major battle. In July, Johnston is relieved by Jefferson Davis, and John Bell Hood replaces him. Hood attacks Sherman several times without success over the course of the next month, and sustains several defeats with heavy losses to his army. A siege follows, which ends when Sherman cuts the last rail line into Atlanta at the end of August. Hood is forced to abandon the city to Sherman on September 2 to avoid being trapped in Atlanta. Altogether, the Atlanta campaign costs the Union 31,000 men, while the Confederates lose 35,000. On November 8, Lincoln wins a second term in office, defeating Democrat George McClellan. His election ends any possibility of a negotiated end to the war that will include the existence of an independent Confederate States of America. Sherman levels Atlanta, burning anything that can possibly be used by the Confederate army, then embarks on his "March to the Sea" (November 15- December 21), cutting his army loose from its supply line, and living off the land. His army chews a 30-mile wide path of destruction through Georgia, destroying railroads, bridges, cotton gins, factories and mills, seizing livestock and burning crops, disrupting the Confederate economy and demoralizing its citizens. The march ends at Savannah, which Sherman offers to Lincoln as a Christmas present after his men occupy it without a fight on December 20. While Sherman has been marching east, Hood has gone north, invading Tennessee after abandoning Atlanta. He attacks a Union army of 55,000 under George Thomas at Nashville on December 15, in a move born of desperation. Hood's army, with only 30,000 men, is crushed, suffering 6000 casualties, and after the Battle of Nashville the Army of Tennessee virtually ceases to exist as a fighting force.

1865

In late January, Sherman with 60,000 men, invades South Carolina, brushing aside feeble opposition, and occupies the state capital, Columbia. Most of the city is destroyed in a fire on the day Sherman's troops capture it, February 17. In Virginia, the siege of Petersburg, which had begun at the end of June, comes to an end on March 25, when Grant's men cut the remaining rail connection into the city. Lee is forced to abandon the defense of Richmond when Petersburg falls, and the Confederate capital is occupied by Union troops on April 3. Lee's army flees to the west, but without supplies or reinforcements, it begins to disintegrate . On April 9, the Army of Northern Virginia, now reduced to 26,000 ragged, starving men, is surrounded at Appomattox Courthouse and forced to surrender. On April 15, Abraham Lincoln is assassinated by John Wilkes Booth. He dies the next day, and Andrew Johnson becomes the 17th President of the United States. On April 26, Joseph Johnston surrenders his forces to Sherman in North Carolina, ending organized resistance east of the Mississippi. On May 10, Jefferson Davis is taken prisoner by Union cavalrymen near Irwinville, Georgia. On June 2, Kirby Smith formally surrenders the Confederate Department of the Trans-Mississippi, ending all formal resistance to the Federal Government.

***

Although the above brief recitation can hardly be considered a definitive history of the Civil War, it will suffice for the purpose of comparing the historical Civil War with the counterfactual you have just read. The point of departure ("POD", to use AH jargon) from our history is of course, the Battle of Antietam, which actually resulted in a draw rather than the destruction of the Army of Northern Virginia.

An absolute prerequisite for any serious counterfactual history is plausibility. In other words, could the POD chosen have reasonably happened in the "alternate" way? The Battle of Antietam is a natural choice for a Civil War POD, because during this battle the Army of Northern Virginia was on the verge of destruction several times, and it is plausible to imagine that it could have ended as it did in this book (unless one is a strict historical determinist, in which case he has no business reading counterfactual histories). Chapter One tracks the historical Battle of Antietam until it reaches the death of Lee. What prevented the battle from ending as described in this counterfactual was the opportune appearance of A.P. Hill with his division at about 3:30, just in time to take Burnside's men in the flank and scotch the final Union threat. Had Hill been a little slower coming up from Harper's Ferry or Burnside's attack a little quicker to develop, there would have been no Army of Northern Virginia left by the time Hill's division arrived at Sharpsburg.

Of course, the POD chosen here hardly exhausts the possibilities for an early Confederate defeat. For example, the Army of Northern Virginia could have been annihilated earlier at Antietam, if McClellan had allowed Franklin to throw VI Corps into the weakened Confederate center after Richardson's men had created a breach there. However, I do not believe this is very plausible, because it would have been so unlikely for McClellan to have acted differently than he actually did, under almost any imaginable stimulus. It would have been asking for the impossible, by requiring Little Mac to act against his very nature.

However, there are other battles where one might plausibly find a different outcome that would have drastically shortened the war. In July, 1863, after the Battle of Gettysburg, for example, Lee's army was trapped against a swollen Potomac River and probably could have been destroyed in *toto* had Meade been willing to force his exhausted men to attack the even more exhausted Confederates.

Likewise, the gods of war must have been smiling on the Confederacy in May of 1864, when Grant managed to bamboozle Lee and land 30,000 men at the gates of Petersburg, with only a skeleton garrison occupying the fortifications opposing them. If the Union commander had been someone other than the bumbling amateur Benjamin Butler, or if the professionals advising Butler had displayed minimal competence, Petersburg and Richmond would have fallen to the Federals then and there, probably shortening the war by six months to a year.

Even Battle of Fredericksburg, rightly considered to be a complete Union disaster, could have easily ended similar to the way it is described here in Chapter Five. Meade's division did in fact walk into a gap in the Confederate line in the historic Battle of Fredericksburg, and if he had been able to communicate his position to I Corps commander John Reynolds in time, the Confederate victory might have turned into a defeat.

The point therefore, is not that the elementary one that the Civil War would have been foreshortened if A.P. Hill had been tardy in arriving at Sharpsburg, the particular counterfactual examined here. Rather, it is that the Southern cause was foredoomed, and that only because of undeserved good fortune was the Confederacy able to survive as long as it did. Why do I say this?

The Civil War was in many ways the harbinger of modern "industrial" warfare. It was the first the first major war in which railroads played an important role, the first to routinely arm their men with rifled firearms, the first to use mass-produced rifled field artillery, the first to have instantaneous communication by telegraph, the first with ironclad warships and so forth. All of these weapons depended to a greater or lesser degree on the industrial capacity of the belligerents. In modern warfare, the outcome of the contest is generally decided by population and industrial capacity, and by ability to efficiently mobilize that capacity.

Or in the words of historian Paul Kennedy [in reference to World War One], "Victory in a prolonged Great Power war usually went to the coalition with the largest productive base." *The Rise and Fall of the Great Powers* (New York, 1989, p.258). Kennedy points out that the population imbalance (North 20,000,000, South 6,000,000 plus 3,000,000 slaves) gave the Confederacy a much smaller pool of potential soldiers. This resulted in the Union being able to field armies totaling approximately 1,000,000 men at peak strength, with 2,000,000 serving at one time or another, while the Confederate army never had more than 450,000 men in service, and only 900,000 ever served at all.

And yet, the South could not even afford to put this lesser number of men into the army without weakening an economy that was already much smaller than its opponent's.. To cite a few examples: in 1860, the value of manufactured goods from the State of New York alone ($300,000) was quadruple that of the total produced by Virginia, Mississippi, Louisiana and Alabama *combined*. The entire Confederacy in that same year produced 36,000 tons of pig iron, while in the same year the State of Pennsylvania alone produced 580,000 tons. And so on.

The Civil War was the first railroad war, and trains proved to be the most important single element in both supplying and moving the armies. In this vital area, the difference between the two sides was stark. The railways of the seceding states aggregated about 9,000 miles of track, much of it flimsy construction that fell to pieces under the strain of heavy use in wartime. Many of the southern lines, moreover, were built primarily to take cotton to the markets rather than as part of a transportation network, and often were had different gauges than neighboring lines, making direct connections and sharing of equipment difficult or impossible. Finally, the locomotives and rolling stock were insufficient in both quantity and quality to meet the needs of either the military or the economy, and the industrial plant of the Confederacy was incapable of either building new ones or manufacturing replacements for worn-out track, or new parts for engines and rolling stock.

On the other hand, the North began the war with a network of 22,000 miles of track, most of it of a single, standard gauge and designed for heavy use. Also, in 1861 the Union had a far greater number of locomotives and larger supply of railcars than did the Confederacy, and the North's superior industrial muscle allowed it to maintain its track, and build new engines and rolling stock during the war.

It is Kennedy's view that the material imbalance between the contestants placed the Confederacy in an insoluble strategic dilemma. Given the far greater population and industrial might of the Union, the rebels could not realistically hope to invade and conquer the North. The only other strategy available to the South, prolonging the war until the Northern public wearied of it, was unlikely to succeed unless the Confederacy either gained the adherence of Maryland and Kentucky or was aided by a massive foreign intervention, neither of which was very likely to happen. Moreover, even if the Confederacy was able to prolong the war, as they did in fact, this was just different road to the same destination. Because of the material disparities between the opposing sides, the longer the war continued, the weaker the South's position would become, in both absolute and relative terms, thereby leading to a Union victory.

Kennedy more or less dismisses the possibility that the South could have won the war, concluding that the North's advantages made the outcome almost a foregone conclusion. (*Rise and Fall*, p.180-182). But it is possible to argue that Kennedy oversimplifies the issue, in that he makes too little allowance for the asymmetrical war aims of the two sides, a factor which reduced the Union's theoretically overwhelming advantages considerably in practice. For the Confederacy to prevail, it did not, after all, need to subdue the United States, but only to endure. If instead of the aggressive "offensive-defense" advocated and practiced by Robert E. Lee, the South could have chosen to fight strictly on the defensive, which would have been far less costly in terms of manpower. If it had chosen to fight this kind of war, this also would have meant that the Rebel armies would have enjoyed short, safe supply lines, rather than long and vulnerable ones. For an example of how a purely defensive, life-saving strategy might have worked, one need only look at the campaign conducted by Joseph Johnston with only 60,000 men against W.T. Sherman's army of 100,000 in the spring and summer of 1864. Sherman was able to advance no more 100 miles in 76 days against his tenacious opponent, and at the end Johnston's army was about the same strength as it had been at the beginning, while after a 2 ½ month campaign, Sherman had gained no important strategic objective.

Contrast this with the lengthy butcher's bill that accompanied even the most dazzling of Lee's victories. The Second Battle of Manassas is regarded as one of Lee's greatest triumphs, resulting in the Federal armies being driven back into the shelter of Washington after having suffered 16,000 casualties as against only slightly more than 9,000 for the Confederates. But too often overlooked is the fact that, relative to the sizes the opposing armies, Second Manassas was a net gain for the Union. The Confederate loss equaled 19 percent of Lee's army, whereas the Federals lost only 13 percent of their men. It does not require a mathematical genius to see that if the Confederacy continued to win such "victories", they would run out of men before the United States did.

On the other side of the coin, in order to win the war, the Union was obliged to occupy virtually all of the territory of the rebellious states, and every additional occupied mile required additional occupation troops who would be unavailable for service on the front lines. In addition, as Union armies penetrated deeper into the South, more and more men were required to guard the lengthening supply lines for those armies, men that could not be used for offensive combat. Buell's abortive Chattanooga campaign in 1862 is a good illustration of how little value the Federal advantages in men and material were when their vulnerable supply lines could not be defended. A few thousand cavalry raiders under Nathan Bedford Forrest were able to bring the advance of a 40,000 man army to a grinding halt, by striking at the latter's exposed communications. Lest it be thought that only mediocre commanders like Buell could be bested in this way, it was Forrest's raids on his supply line which brought Grant's first Vicksburg campaign to an untimely end, and Grant was arguably the Union's best general.

The task for the United States in April 1861 has been compared to that which faced Great Britain in subduing the rebellious colonies in1775:

[Great Britain had] to reassert its authority over a vast territorial empire...with a dearth of strategically decisive types of objectives whose seizure could produce disproportionate economic, political or moral results. In both instances, the rebels began their war in substantial control of their territory, and needed only to conduct a successful defense of what they already held to win. The established government had the much more difficult feat of conquest. In both instances, the prospect was further encumbered by the limitations of conquest by the bayonet as an instrument for securing the desired renewal of political allegiance.

(*The American Way of War*, Russell Weigley , New York, 1973, p.92)

Weigley goes on to suggest that had the South adopted George Washington's strategy, which emphasized the preservation of his army above any other consideration, it might have been able to outlast it's larger opponent.

Contrariwise, it should be recalled that the Thirteen Colonies did not gain their independence without outside help. It is likely that the War of Independence could not have been won without the aid of France, and it is all but certain that victory at the climactic Battle of Yorktown would not have been possible without Admiral DeGrasse's victory over Sir Thomas Graves in the Battle of the Chesapeake and the blockade of Cornwallis' troops by the French fleet. Also missing from Weigley's analysis is any consideration of the importance of industrial capacity in the mid-19th century compared to the latter 18th. It is inconceivable that the South could maintain an army in the field without the any source of ammunition, without railroads to bring up rations, clothing, weapons, tents, wagon wheels, caissons and all the other manufactured necessities of industrialized warfare, which would have happened if the Federal armies had been allowed to occupy Atlanta, Richmond and the handful of other Confederate industrial centers. Once these cities were in Union hands, the war would have been over within a few weeks at most. This was very unlike the situation that obtained in the Revolutionary War, when the British occupation of Philadelphia, New York, Boston and Charleston had little or no effect on the combat effectiveness of the colonial armies, who were not dependent on supplies from the cities.

All of which leaves us back where we started, which is to say that, based on relative size and economic power of the two adversaries, and without some substantial foreign intervention and/or a massive failure of Federal leadership , the South never truly had a chance to win the Civil War.

On Sources

Although this book is a work of fiction, it is fiction with a serious purpose, and I attempted to write it as I would an actual history. Many of the *shorter* quotations in this book were the actual words of the persons cited, as for example Lincoln's remark about McClellan's affinity for the stationary engine, or Halleck's letter to Rosecrans although source cited was from my imagination.

Some of the "primary source" material was adapted from actual statements. I have always loved the Gettysburg Address, but since there was no Battle of Gettysburg in this book, I decided to salvage some of this immortal speech, and put it in the mouth of Jefferson Davis. I also took the liberty of using the names of real authors for some of my invented books in the name of authenticity, for example, naming Russell Weigley (real), as the author of *The Generals of the Confederacy: A Study in Command* (not real. I wish he had written it, though: I would have liked to read it.)

Most of the block quotes from the memoirs and letters of eyewitnesses were of my own coining. I did my best to make the grammar, syntax and vocabulary as authentic as possible, and labored to make the eyewitness accounts of the fighting resemble those of genuine eyewitnesses. To the extent my fictions were convincing, they may have engendered a certain amount of confusion for the reader. If you decided, for instance, that you wanted to read Bruce Catton's biography of George McClellan, *The Reluctant Warrior*, which I cited in Chapter Two or his book about the Army of the Potomac's 1863 campaign, *One More River to Cross* in Chapter Three, you would be out of luck, as these are titles I invented for books that do not have any corporeal existence.

If only to clear up at least some of the confusion alluded to above, although I did not believe it was either necessary or practical to cite every (real) source) individually, I thought that a short bibliographic essay might be helpful. It might also be useful for anyone wishing to further pursue some of the issues raised in this book, by writing a book refuting my arguments.

In addition to the general sources cited below, I found Bruce Catton's "Crisis at Antietam" (*American Heritage*, August, 1958) particularly helpful in my description of the Battle of Sharpsburg (Antietam). I am also fortunate enough to live within a half-day's drive of many of the famous Civil War battlefields, including the beautifully preserved Antietam National Battlefield, and was privileged to see for myself the Cornfield, Bloody Lane and Burnside's Bridge, while the ghostly clamor of battle sounded in my imagination. If you have any interest in the Civil War, I highly recommend taking the time to visit the park. The website is: (http://www.nps.gov/anti/index.htm).

For my account of the Battle of Chickasaw Bayou in Chapter Three, the website of the 16th Ohio Volunteer Infantry http:/www.mkwe.com/home.htm was of great assistance

The website of the Civil War Trust was an important resource that was used many times throughout this book, and particularly as to the Battle of Fredericksburg (http:/www.civilwar.org/battlefields/fredericksburg.html.)

Chapter Seven is entirely factual, and the citations therein are all genuine. Representative Julian's entire speech was printed in the *Congressional Globe*, January 14, 1862 , p. 328-332, and is made available on line by the Library of Congress at its American Memory website (http://memory.loc.gov/ammem/amlaw/lwcg.html).

Lincoln's famous open letter to Horace Greeley is available in full from many sources, including http:/www.civilwarhome.com/lincolngreeley.html The autobiography of the oft-maligned Benjamin Butler cited herein is available in full from the Internet Archives (https://archive.org/details/ autobiographyper0192butl). A wealth of information on the Confiscation Acts, the Emancipation Proclamation, the recruiting of African-American soldiers and related topics can be found at the website Mr. Lincoln and Freedom http://www.mrlincolnandfreedom.org, a project of the Lehrman Institute and the Lincoln Institute.

In Chapter Eight, the two quotes from the anonymous New York Times reporter describing the notorious "mud march" are genuine. The original article was reprinted in *The Rebellion Record*, Volume 6, a vast, multi-volume collection of articles, letters eyewitness accounts and more from the Civil War, provided in digital form through the good offices of the Internet Archives. See: https://archive.org/details/bub_gb_Xi8OAAAAIAAJ . The account by Warren Lee Goss is taken from *Recollections of a Private: A Story of the Army of the Potomac* (New York, 1890), p.137. The entire book is reproduced digitally and made available by Google Books at : (http://books.google.com/books?id=mAFIFXCAkdUC& printsec=frontcover&source=gbs_ge_summary_r&cad= 0#v=onepage&q&f=false).

The passage from Dolly Sumner Lunt's *A Woman's Wartime Journal* (New York, 1918) in Chapter Nine was actually written about Sherman's March to the Sea, and took place in Georgia rather than Mississippi, but since the March to the Sea never occurs in Jack's history, and the descriptions seemed otherwise appropriate, I included it, substituting Grant for Sherman and otherwise leaving it unchanged. Lunt's book is provided by University of North Carolina on that institution's website Documenting the South (http://docsouth.unc.edu/fpn/burge/lunt.html). The source of the famous Frederick Douglass quote, which I assumed would be easy to find, turned into a long hunt. Although literally dozens of books and websites use the quote, most either simply stated that Douglass wrote it, without any further attribution, or (more commonly) said nothing at all about the source. I was beginning to wonder if Douglass had actually written (or spoken) these words at all, when finally I tracked down my prey in the Library of Congress' website. For the record, it was part of a speech he gave at a rally at National Hall, Philadelphia, July 6, 1863. (http://www.loc.gov/resource/mfd.22007/?sp=7).

The description in Chapter Ten of the burning of Richmond from the June 1865 issue of the *Atlantic Monthly* can be read in full at Old Magazine Articles (http://www.oldmagazinearticles.com/eyewitness_to_the_fall_of_Richmond_Virginia_1865#.VNbKICyrHfe). Although the passage in the book does not indicate it, the overall tone of the piece strongly suggests that the anonymous observer was a Union man, who could hardly contain his glee as he watched the destruction of the Rebel capital. The Joseph Johnston quote is taken verbatim from his memoirs, *Narrative of Military Operations* (New York, 1874), which is made available in through the good offices of the Internet Archives https://archive.org/details/narrativemilita01johngoog.

As a resource for technical details of Civil War field works, Lt. Colonel David C. Chuber's Master's thesis, *Field Fortifications During the Civil War* (Ft. Leavenworth, 1996), cannot be improved upon. It may be downloaded in pdf form from: www.dtic.mil/cgi-bin/GetTRDoc?AD=ADA313032, and I recommend it to anyone who wishes to gain a better understanding of the tactics used by both sides during sieges and positional warfare in the Civil War.

It would have been impossible for me to kept the numbers and unit sizes in the various fictional battles straight without repeated reference to Formations and Ranks in Civil War Units http://www.angelfire.com/wv/wasec5/formations.html, for which I thank Webmaster, Mr. Hal Sharpe.

For general background, I relied chiefly on standard accounts of the Civil War. James M. McPherson's *Battle Cry of Freedom* (New York, 1988), provided coverage of the economic, political and social dimensions of the war as well as covering the battles, and did so in a single volume. I can heartily recommend it even to those who are already familiar with the military aspects of the Civil War. Also in constant use during the writing of this book was Shelby Foote's excellent three-volume *The Civil War: A Narrative* (New York, 1974), particularly the last two volumes. Likewise, Bruce Catton's three-volume *Centennial History of the Civil War* (New York, 1963) and *The Army of the Potomac* (New York,1953) remained on the desk next to my P.C. at all times, until I finally completed this book.

On Nomenclature

The Union army used a fairly straightforward numerical system for its units, with the army corps having unique numbers, designated in Roman numerals (i.e., IV Corps, XII Corps etc.), the various components then bearing consecutive numbers starting at one (for example, the X Corps would have First and Second Divisions, which would in turn contain First and Second Brigades, and so on). The regiments were named for the state from which they came, and numbered by the date order in which they were raised (62nd New York).

Although the Confederate army started the war using a similar system to that of the Union, this was soon superseded by a less formal method of naming the various units after their commanding officers (the Stonewall Brigade, Cleburne's Division, etc.). These names would remain even after the original commanding officer had moved on, thus creating great potential for confusion, when students of the Civil War are confronted by phrases like: "Cleburne's Division (now commanded by Brigadier General Lucius Polk)."

I should note here that the all the characters in the main narrative are real historical personages(which is not true of all of the sources of the quotes, such as Reverend Lorch in Chapter One), and their ranks and units in the story are, for the most part, exactly the ones they had in history. The exceptions are those necessitated by the plot, since as a result of the changed outcome of Antietam, many Confederate units were moved, and their officers killed, captured, transferred, promoted, and so forth. In cases where the plot obliged me to make changes from the historical record, for example, by promoting a colonel to brigadier general, I would try to fill the vacancy with a subordinate officer from a regiment that was in the same brigade. Even in these cases, the man chosen was a genuine historical personage.

Many battles of the Civil War have two names, one used by the South and one by the North. The Union often named battles after nearby streams (Antietam, Bull Run) or other natural features (South Mountain, Pea Ridge), while the Confederates generally used a nearby town (Sharpsburg, Manassas, Boonesboro). Being a Yankee from Pennsylvania, I used the Northern names except where I was quoting a Southern source.

Andrew J. Heller
Erdenheim, PA
April, 2018